What will happen to Sterling and her new foal?

"Any special instructions?" Samantha asked.

"Just keep an eye on her and give me a call when it looks like things are getting close," the vet directed her.

Allie watched her walk away, then turned to Samantha. "What do you need me to do now?" she asked.

"You can bring the other horses in," Samantha said. "We'll get chores taken care of early, and I'll call Chris to see if she wants to come over and do foal watch with us."

Allie was relieved. With Christina's training in veterinary medicine, it would be good to have her on hand, just in case of an emergency.

Allie left the barn to start bringing the rest of the horses in, while Samantha went to her office to call Christina.

When Allie went around the barn with Sterling's lead in hand, she stopped dead. The mare's turnout was empty. Allie saw the broken board lying on the ground outside the stall, and she stared for a minute, absorbing what she could see had happened. Sterling had gone over the fence. Allie looked around frantically, but there was no sign of the big gray mare. Sterling, who was due to drop her foal at any time, was gone!

Collect all the books in the Thoroughbred series

#1 *A Horse Called Wonder*
#2 *Wonder's Promise*
#3 *Wonder's First Race*
#4 *Wonder's Victory*
#5 *Ashleigh's Dream*
#6 *Wonder's Yearling*
#7 *Samantha's Pride*
#8 *Sierra's Steeplechase*
#9 *Pride's Challenge*
#10 *Pride's Last Race*
#11 *Wonder's Sister*
#12 *Shining's Orphan*
#13 *Cindy's Runaway Colt*
#14 *Cindy's Glory*
#15 *Glory's Triumph*
#16 *Glory in Danger*
#17 *Ashleigh's Farewell*
#18 *Glory's Rival*
#19 *Cindy's Heartbreak*
#20 *Champion's Spirit*
#21 *Wonder's Champion*
#22 *Arabian Challenge*
#23 *Cindy's Honor*
#24 *The Horse of Her Dreams*
#25 *Melanie's Treasure*
#26 *Sterling's Second Chance*
#27 *Christina's Courage*
#28 *Camp Saddlebrook*
#29 *Melanie's Last Ride*
#30 *Dylan's Choice*
#31 *A Home for Melanie*
#32 *Cassidy's Secret*
#33 *Racing Parker*
#34 *On the Track*
#35 *Dead Heat*
#36 *Without Wonder*
#37 *Star in Danger*
#38 *Down to the Wire*
#39 *Living Legend*
#40 *Ultimate Risk*
#41 *Close Call*
#42 *The Bad-Luck Filly*
#43 *Fallen Star*
#44 *Perfect Image*
#45 *Star's Chance*
#46 *Racing Image*
#47 *Cindy's Desert Adventure*
#48 *Cindy's Bold Start*
#49 *Rising Star*
#50 *Team Player*
#51 *Distance Runner*
#52 *Perfect Challenge*
#53 *Derby Fever*
#54 *Cindy's Last Hope*
#55 *Great Expectations*
#56 *Hoofprints in the Snow*
#57 *Faith in a Long Shot*
#58 *Christina's Shining Star*
#59 *Star's Inspiration*
#60 *Taking the Reins*
#61 *Parker's Passion*
#62 *Unbridled Fury*
#63 *Starstruck*
#64 *The Price of Fame*
#65 *Bridal Dreams*
#66 *Samantha's Irish Luck*
#67 *Breaking the Fall*
#68 *Kaitlin's Wild Ride*
#69 *Melanie's Double Jinx*
#70 *Allie's Legacy*
#71 *Calamity Jinx*
#72 *Legacy's Gift*

Collect all the books in the Ashleigh series

#1 *Lightning's Last Hope*
#2 *A Horse for Christmas*
#3 *Waiting for Stardust*
#4 *Good-bye, Midnight Wanderer*
#5 *The Forbidden Stallion*
#6 *A Dangerous Ride*
#7 *Derby Day*
#8 *The Lost Foal*
#9 *Holiday Homecoming*
#10 *Derby Dreams*
#11 *Ashleigh's Promise*
#12 *Winter Race Camp*
#13 *The Prize*
#14 *Ashleigh's Western Challenge*
#15 *Stardust's Foal*

THOROUGHBRED Super Editions

Ashleigh's Christmas Miracle
Ashleigh's Diary
Ashleigh's Hope
Samantha's Journey

ASHLEIGH'S Thoroughbred Collection

Star of Shadowbrook Farm
The Forgotten Filly
Battlecry Forever!

THOROUGHBRED

Legacy's Gift

CREATED BY
JOANNA CAMPBELL
WRITTEN BY
MARY NEWHALL

HarperEntertainment
An Imprint of HarperCollins*Publishers*

HarperEntertainment
An Imprint of HarperCollins*Publishers*
10 East 53rd Street, New York, NY 10022-5299

Produced by 17th Street Productions, an Alloy Online, Inc., company

HarperCollins books are available at special quantity discounts for bulk purchases for sales promotions, premiums, or fund-raising. For information please call or write: Special Markets Department, HarperCollins Publishers, 10 East 53rd Street, New York, NY 10022-5299. Telephone: (212) 207-7528. Fax: (212) 207-7222.

ISBN 0-06-078117-3

First printing: July 2005

Printed in the United States of America

Visit HarperEntertainment on the World Wide Web at www.harpercollins.com

10 9 8 7 6 5 4 3 2 1

For my beautiful, talented daughter Danielle,
with loving memories of Flame and Santana,
two of the greatest horses we've ever known

Legacy's Gift

1

"ARE YOU NERVOUS?" CINDY MCLEAN ASKED, LOOKING UP at sixteen-year-old Allison Avery. Allie was seated astride Charming Miss, a three-year-old bay Thoroughbred filly, in the viewing paddock at Kentucky's Keeneland racetrack. The cool October air was filled with the sounds of the fans at the track for a Saturday afternoon of racing.

Allie, proudly wearing Tall Oaks' green-and-purple racing silks, grinned down at her foster mother. "Just a little," she said in response to Cindy's question. "If Charming and I win this race, I'll have the forty-five wins I need to get rid of my bug, and Charming will break her maiden."

As an apprentice jockey, Allie's name on the racing program was marked with an asterisk, or "bug," to show that she wasn't a fully licensed jockey.

Cindy nodded thoughtfully. "Then you'll just need to have a complete year of racing behind you and you'll be a full-fledged jockey."

After becoming an apprentice jockey the day after her sixteenth birthday, Allie had enjoyed an impressive series of wins over the past three months. On this day, at the start of the fall meet at Keeneland, she was determined that she was going to have another successful race.

"Charming and I are going to tear up the track today." She patted the filly's sleek neck. "Aren't we, girl?"

From where she stood, holding Charming's lead while Allie finished a quick check of her equipment, Beckie Dauti, the Australian groom who worked as the filly's handler, nodded in agreement. "I know you two are going to give Tall Oaks a memorable win today, Allie. Get lucky, mate."

"Go get 'em, tiger," Cindy said, patting Allie's knee

as Beckie led the prancing filly toward the track and the escort riders.

Allie saw several people she knew standing near the viewing paddock rail. Ashleigh Griffen, the famous jockey and a close family friend, stood beside Samantha Nelson, Cindy's older sister. Samantha had twenty-month-old Leah balanced on her hip. Leah had inherited her mother's thick red hair and blue eyes, and she waved a chubby hand excitedly at Allie. Beside Samantha, twenty-year-old Christina Reese, Ashleigh's daughter, held Leah's twin brother. Luke was a handsome blond, just like his father, Tor Nelson. Christina, an experienced jockey, grinned at Allie, who waved at the group. Nearby, Allie's best friend, Lila Wilson, was standing with her parents. Lila, who had helped prepare Charming for the race, was wearing jeans and paddock boots, but Senator Wilson, her father, was clad in a dark suit, looking very official. At the end of the race, the Wilsons would be in the winner's circle, as the senator had been asked to present the purse to the winning owner.

"Good luck!" Christina called out, waving with her free hand.

"See you in the winner's circle," Lila called, making a V for victory.

Allie touched her hand to her riding helmet in a brief salute, then she and Charming Miss headed onto the track, jogging past the grandstand in the pre-race warm-up and post parade. She watched the four fillies in line in front of them, all fit and energetic, and she leaned forward in the saddle. "They're going to be watching your tail in a minute or two," she murmured to Charming. The filly flicked her ears back in response to the sound of Allie's voice, and as if she understood, she pranced a little more, tugging at the hold the pony rider had on her lead.

It hardly felt like two years had passed since Allie, as a fourteen-year-old orphan, had left California for Kentucky and life at Tall Oaks, the prestigious Thoroughbred farm that Cindy owned with her husband, Ben al-Rihani. But Allie had soon adjusted to the changes the move had brought, and time seemed to fly by. All of the memories Allie had collected during the last couple of years were good ones.

Beneath her, she felt Charming tense up and give a little kick with her hind legs. Allie stroked the filly's neck, letting the racehorse break into a collected canter next to the trotting quarter horse the pony rider was on. "Save your best for the race, girl," Allie admonished the filly, who tossed her head defiantly as they followed the lead horses behind the starting gate.

Allie glanced around at the rest of the Thoroughbreds listed on the race program, watching their attitudes and behavior as they milled around behind the gate, waiting for their turn to be loaded. The number three horse was fighting the gate crew, balking about entering the tiny chute. Two burly crew members locked their hands behind the filly's hindquarters and forced her into the box. Allie exhaled with relief when the filly didn't rear up or flip over to keep from going in. She and Cindy had put a lot of time into Charming's training, getting the filly comfortable with loading into the gate easily, but Allie knew some trainers didn't put a lot of effort into that part of racing. What was most important to them was just getting the high-strung horse onto the track so it could run.

Cindy had learned to handle Thoroughbreds as a youngster when she was living at Whitebrook, the Thoroughbred farm owned by Ashleigh Griffen and her husband, Mike Reese. Like Mike and Ashleigh, she believed that the less stressful the minutes before the race were, the more focus and energy the horse would have on the track. So far that attitude had worked well for the horses at both Whitebrook and Tall Oaks. As proud as she was to be riding for Tall Oaks, Allie was equally happy to wear Whitebrook's blue-and-white silks when she rode for the other farm.

Soon she and Charming were in their chute, waiting for the rest of the eleven fillies to load so that the race could begin. The murmured voices of the jockeys on either side of her carried over the sound of the nervous racehorses, who shifted and stomped in the tight confines of their gates, waiting impatiently to burst onto the track. Beneath Allie, Charming pawed a furrow into the footing and took in a long, snorting breath. "Easy, girl," Allie said quietly. "Any minute now."

"One back!" When she heard the familiar call that indicated there was only one horse left to load, Allie shifted her weight over Charming's powerful shoulders, collected fistfuls of mane along with the reins, braced her feet against the stirrups, and prepared for the explosive start of the race.

After a few more tense seconds, the row of gates sprang open, and Charming leaped onto the track with the rest of the field. As if they were one, the horses pressed to the left, toward the inside rail, and Allie darted quick looks around her, sizing up the placing of the horses, watching for the jockeys and mounts that she knew presented the biggest challenges.

Being an apprentice jockey meant that most of the other jockeys didn't hold her in very high regard. And Allie knew that at times their attitude was justified. Without the experience of years of racing behind them, apprentices were the jockeys most likely to make mistakes on the track, interfering with other horses or, even worse, causing terrible wrecks.

"It's a tough spot to be in," Cindy had told Allie before her first race. "The older jocks don't want you on the track without lots of experience, but you can't get the experience without being on the track."

Allie understood, and she was prepared to lose races before she'd risk her mount or the safety of any of the other riders.

But astride an experienced four-year-old Thoroughbred owned by Ghyllian Hollis's Celtic Meadows farm, Allie had won her first race. She knew the win wasn't completely due to her fantastic skill as a jockey—she'd been given a talented horse to ride. She knew that when jockeys like her own mother, Jilly

Gordon—not to mention Ashleigh and Cindy—had started racing, the only horses they could get were the long shots. But women jockeys had proven themselves capable, earning respect and good mounts over the years. Allie felt lucky to be riding now, instead of when it had been so much tougher for women jockeys.

As the field of eleven raced along the track, Allie found herself blocked in, caught on the rail, with the number seven filly to her right and three racehorses directly in front of them. She stifled a groan. Beneath her, Charming was running easily, but Allie could feel frustration building up in the filly as the lead horses kept her from moving into a faster pace.

There was a tiny opening between the front horse and the rail, and Allie considered it for a fleeting second. But the space was too narrow. It was too risky a move, and she resigned herself to the idea that if they lost, they lost. She wasn't going to take a chance of hurting Charming in order to try for a win, as much as she'd love to bring the filly to the wire in first place.

As they came into the first turn of the track, two furlongs into the six-furlong race, the filly beside them dropped back, and Allie quickly shifted her weight, urging Charming through the gap the filly had left. Now they were on the outside, moving up beside the three front-runners.

"You can do this, girl," Allie urged Charming. "I know you've got it in you to pass them all." While Charming Miss wasn't nearly the caliber of racehorse as her stablemate, a chestnut filly called Alpine Meadow, Allie had worked with Charming enough to know her strengths. She didn't have enough staying power to run a full mile, but she could turn on the speed during the last two furlongs of a six-furlong race and blow the competition away. And a fast track was her favorite footing to run on.

They moved out of the last curve of the track and onto the straight stretch, and Allie watched Charming flick her ears, angling her head as though she was sizing up the competition.

"Now, girl!" Allie cried, shifting her hands up Charming's outstretched neck. Beneath her, she felt the filly switch gears, and in a few strides they were even with the lead horses. The filly on the rail dropped back, drained from the effort she had put into keeping up such a grueling pace, and Charming nosed ahead of the other two Thoroughbreds.

Beside her, Allie heard the jockey aboard the number two horse, a big black filly, smack his whip on the racehorse's hip. The filly snapped her head up and dug her hooves into the track, straining to maintain her pace.

But as they closed in on the finish line, Allie knew that Charming was solidly in first place. They crossed the finish line a full length ahead of the second-place horse, and Allie couldn't resist letting out a joyful whoop. She slowed Charming and circled the filly back, jogging her to where Cindy and Beckie waited on the track, broad grins stretched across their faces.

"You did it!" Beckie exclaimed, catching Charming's headstall. Allie bounced to the ground, and Cindy swept her up in an enthusiastic hug.

"You and Charming were awesome," Cindy said, her eyes bright. "You're an incredible jockey, Allie."

Allie smiled back at her foster mother. "Thanks to a great teacher," she replied, then turned to pulled Charming's saddle off her back.

The filly's coat was dark with sweat, and Cindy pressed her hand against Charming's muscular chest. "She's barely winded," she said, then tilted her head toward the winner's circle. "Let's get you weighed in and let the photographers do their thing, then we can cool her out and head home."

Allie carried the saddle over to where the clerk of the scales waited. "That's it," the man said with a nod after he had checked her weight. "You're good to go."

Allie crossed the circle to where Cindy and Beckie were standing with the Wilsons and Charming.

"You guys rock!" Lila said, giving Allie a high five. "I knew you'd win."

"Thanks," Allie said, letting Lila boost her back onto Charming for the quick ceremony.

Senator Wilson shook hands with Cindy, then smiled up at Allie. "I'm glad they asked me to officiate for the race," he told Allie. "I couldn't be more pleased for Tall Oaks, and for you."

"I was afraid you were going to stay boxed in for the whole race," Mrs. Wilson said to Allie. "I had my fingers crossed the entire time."

"Except when she was grabbing my shoulder and yelling, 'Do you see what she's doing? Do you see?' " Lila added dryly, giving her mother a teasing grin.

"It was exciting," Mrs. Wilson said with a laugh. "I love watching the races, especially when the horse I'm cheering for is the winner."

After the group posed for the track photographer, Allie slipped from Charming's back again, and while Beckie took the filly to the vet's barn for the required drug testing, Allie headed for the jockeys' lounge to change out of her silks.

By the time she returned to Charming's stall, Beckie had the filly in the cross ties, getting her ready for the drive home, while Lila helped Cindy pack up the tack.

During the short trip back to Tall Oaks, Cindy talked about the schedule for the rest of the Keeneland meet. "I know Ghyllian Hollis has a couple of horses for you to race, and I'm sure Whitebrook can use you, too. Christina's college schedule is keeping her hopping, and now that Melanie has decided to take some classes, Dad needs another jockey on a regular basis."

Cindy's adoptive father, Ian McLean, was the head trainer at Whitebrook. Melanie Graham, Christina's cousin, had finally started taking college classes after focusing on racing for the two years since she had graduated from high school. Melanie still rode regularly, but she had finally realized that she needed to plan for a future beyond racing, and she was taking a few classes to see what interested her most.

When they arrived at Tall Oaks, Cindy parked the truck near the barn where the horses in training were kept, and while Allie put Charming in her stall, Lila and Beckie unloaded the equipment.

Before she walked to the main barn, Allie detoured to her own Thoroughbred's stall. Wonder's Legacy, the big chestnut stallion Ben and Cindy had given her during her first year at Tall Oaks, nickered a greeting. Allie wrapped her arms around the horse's neck, inhaling deeply. "I won another race, boy," she told him. "Next summer I'll be a real jockey." She stroked his neck. "Before long, I'll be able to race your foals."

Although with his bloodlines Legacy should have been a dynamite racer, he had never gotten much of a chance on the track. His sire, Gold Legacy, had been a great-grandson of the famed Nasrullah, whose bloodlines ran in many of the greatest racehorses in Triple Crown history. Legacy's dam, Ashleigh's Wonder, had also produced several exceptional racehorses. Ben and Cindy's Triple Crown–winning stallion, Wonder's Champion, was one of them. Another of her foals, Wonder's Pride, had won both the Kentucky Derby and the Preakness, while Christina's stallion, Wonder's Star, had won the Belmont. Several of Wonder's other foals had set track records up and down the East Coast.

Allie hoped that Legacy would pass his excellent breeding on to his own offspring. One of the mares he had covered the previous spring was Sterling Dream, a jumper owned by Samantha and Tor. Allie could hardly wait until spring, when the foal would be on the ground.

"I'd better get going," she told Legacy, giving him one last pet. "It's been a long day."

She hurried through the barn, but as she neared Cindy's office, the aisle was dark. She slowed, looking around curiously. Suddenly the lights came on, and a group of people standing in the shadows called out, "Surprise!" Allie jumped, then started to laugh as she read the sign hung in the middle of the aisle: Welcome to Tall Oaks, a Bug-Free Zone.

All the people she had seen at the track were there, along with Ian McLean, his wife, Beth, and their son, Kevin. Melanie was there, as well as Christina's boyfriend, Parker Townsend.

"A party?" Allie asked as her friends crowded around her, clapping her on the back, shaking her hand, and making jokes about not needing any more bug spray.

"Check it out," Elizabeth, the head groom, said, pointing at a table set up against the wall of Cindy's office. "Luis was so determined to have a party, no matter how the race went today, that he even baked a special cake."

As Allie started toward the table, Ben al-Rihani, Cindy's husband of six months, came into the barn. "Allison," he called, and she hurried over to him.

"You didn't do all this for me, did you?" she asked, gazing up at the tall, dark-haired man.

"You deserve it," Ben said with a smile. "And I have to give most of the credit to Elizabeth, Beckie, and Luis. They came up with the idea while I was in New York this past week. I was just happy to get home in time for the party." He squeezed her shoulders as he looked down at her. "I am so proud of you for what you've accomplished, Ala. Cindy and I both are."

At the use of the special nickname, Allie felt a warm glow that had nothing to do with winning the race, or even the party. Ben had explained to her that in Arabic, Ala meant "gift," and he made it clear that he felt she was a special gift to both Cindy and him.

"Congratulations!" Allie glanced past Ben to see Luis, Ben's chef, hurrying into the barn carrying a large tray loaded with little sandwiches. He winked at Allie, a broad grin on his round face. "I get to cook for the greatest jockey Tall Oaks has ever seen." He nodded toward the table. "Did you see your special cake, Allie? Never have I catered a party in the barn, but for you, I would do anything." He looked around the barn. "I can't believe how clean this place is!"

Allie stifled a laugh. If Luis knew how hard the staff worked at cleaning and caring for the barn and horses, he wouldn't have thought twice about serving food there.

Luis gestured for Allie to follow him. "You must see the cake." He grinned. "It is by far my most creative dessert."

She followed the chef to the table and burst out laughing when she saw that Luis had fashioned the cake to look like a giant insect, complete with eyes and legs. "It's perfect," she said, giving the pleased chef a quick hug. "You are brilliant, Luis."

The chef nodded seriously. "I am an artist with food," he said, standing as tall as his stocky frame would allow. He gestured at the cake. "Now we will devour the bug, and it will be no more!"

People crowded around Allie again while Luis and

Christina filled glasses with sparkling cider to distribute to everyone.

"I'd like to make a toast," Ian said loudly when everyone had a glass in hand, with the exception of Luke and Leah. The twins each had a lidded plastic cup to sip from, and the toddlers had begun drinking their juice before Ian finished speaking. He glanced at his grandchildren and shook his head. "I'd better make it quick," he added, then turned to Allie. "An Irish jockey's toast, if you will," he said. "May the best race of your past be the worst race of your future."

"Hear, hear!" Everyone raised their glasses, and amid laughter and talk about Thoroughbred racing, people began filling plates and enjoying Luis's food.

Allie stood back for a minute, watching the cheerful gathering, amazed by the outpouring of affection all these people had for her.

"Are you surprised?" Lila asked, coming up to her with a plate full of hors d'oeuvres.

Allie nodded, afraid she would get emotional if she tried to say anything.

"We jockeys all remember the races that got rid of our bugs," Cindy said as she joined the girls, her own plate loaded with food. "We wanted to make yours especially memorable."

"You have," Allie said. "I'll never forget any of this." As people came up to congratulate her, she felt a warm glow fill her, and her smile grew so wide it hurt her face, but she couldn't stop it. *I have such a wonderful life,* she thought, looking around at the happy gathering. *How did I get so lucky?*

2

"THAT WAS AN AWESOME PARTY," LILA TOLD ALLIE WHEN they met in front of their lockers at Henry Clay High School on Monday morning. "Too bad we can't have one of those every time you win a race."

"I'll suggest it to Cindy and Ben," Allie replied with a laugh. "But I know what the odds are without even asking."

"Zero to nothing," Lila added knowingly. "Did Cindy see your midterm report yet?" she asked, grabbing her English book from her locker. "I'll be glad when we get through algebra. That class is killing my grade point average."

Allie hesitated before answering. She knew Lila struggled with math, and she didn't want to sound like a brainiac, but so far she was getting a solid 4.0 average. "Math isn't my top favorite subject, either," she said, getting her science book out. "I like chemistry lots better."

Lila wrinkled her nose and shook her head. "Give me English any day of the week," she said. "That and physical education are the only thing saving my grade right now."

"Speaking of classes," Allie said, "I'd better get going. See you at lunch?"

"You got it," Lila replied, and the girls hurried off to their first-period classes.

After school, Allie walked past the line of waiting buses and into the student parking area. When she had turned sixteen and gotten her driver's license, Ben and Cindy had agreed that it would be a good idea for her to have her own transportation. Allie enjoyed the freedom of having use of the small sedan they had bought her, but she respected the responsibility that went along with it. It was nice to get home without making the slow trip on the bus with its frequent stops. She was able to help more at the barn, and spend more time with Legacy and the racehorses in training.

But this afternoon, instead of going straight home, she had a detour to make. She drove through the countryside, past the rolling fields of bluegrass, the gracious mansions, and the massive barns, turning onto a gravel drive that wound up a slight rise. The horses in the pastures at Whisperwood were sturdier-looking than the Thoroughbreds at Tall Oaks, heavier-boned, with broad chests and flat knees. Allie admired the well-bred jumpers as she drove past them—tall, athletic-looking animals with long, muscular necks, all of them groomed to perfection.

When Christina had called Allie, inviting her to the farm for a special announcement, Allie wondered if Christina and Parker were going to tell her they had gotten engaged. That, she thought, would be the greatest news in the world. Parker and Christina had treated her like a little sister when she had first come to Lexington, helping her through the difficult times she had had adjusting to so many traumatic changes in her life.

When Whisperwood's barn came into view, Allie saw Samantha standing near the outdoor arena. The slender redhead, clad in jeans and paddock boots, her hands thrust into the pockets of her windbreaker, was watching a blond girl working a big bay horse over some low jumps. Allie pulled up by the indoor arena, parking next to Christina's SUV and Parker Townsend's pickup. Although she was impatient to hear whatever news Christina and Parker had to share, she walked over to Samantha rather than going straight to the barn. Tor and Samantha, along with so many other people, had helped her adjust to her new life in Kentucky, and she couldn't just ignore Samantha.

"Where are Luke and Leah?" she asked, glancing around curiously.

Samantha didn't take her eyes off her young student, but she tilted her head toward the barn. "They're napping in my office," she said. "Kaitlin is keeping an eye on them while she does some filing for me." She flashed a bright smile at Allie. "Whisperwood is getting busier every day, and that means more paperwork to take care of. I'm glad Kaitlin likes office work, because it drives me nuts!"

Kaitlin Boyce, one of Samantha's longtime students, helped out at the farm to cover her tuition for advanced riding lessons.

"Lighten up on the reins, Melody," Samantha called

to the girl in the arena. "Not so much pressure on Orion's mouth."

Allie watched the girl respond to Samantha's instructions, taking the bay over another low jump, then nodded in approval. "She has a good seat," she commented. Allie had spent several years taking lessons in combined training, and she recognized the young rider's potential.

"She's making great progress," Samantha replied, turning her attention to Allie. "I miss having you help out with the lessons. I could use a good riding instructor if you want a job. Parker's pretty busy."

For the last several years Parker had worked at Whisperwood when he wasn't away competing with his eventing horses or training with the other members of the United States Equestrian Team. Parker's expertise and status as a competitor, as well as his way of working with the young students, made him a popular teacher at the farm.

Allie knew that Parker's parents, Brad and Lavinia Townsend, were unhappy that Parker's sport of choice was eventing. The wealthy owners of Townsend Acres, one of the oldest and most prestigious Thoroughbred farms in the area, could easily have helped their son in his dream of competing for Olympic gold, but it seemed as though they had done everything they could to make it difficult for him. Even though Parker had to work hard to make ends meet on his own, he knew that if he had gotten help from his parents, he'd have paid a price for it, and he was happier being independent of them.

"I'm pretty busy at Tall Oaks," Allie said with a grin. "Besides, I'm a better jockey than a jumping teacher." Although Allie's parents, Craig Avery and Jilly Gordon, had both been jockeys, they had urged her to pursue eventing, and Allie had struggled to honor their wishes. But in her heart she had known she was meant to be on the track, and with the help and support of all the people she knew in Kentucky, she was succeeding.

"Your mom and dad would be very proud of how well you're doing," Samantha said. "We're all very proud of you."

"Thanks," Allie said, then glanced toward the barn. "Is Parker done with his afternoon classes?"

Samantha nodded. "He and Chris are clearing the indoor arena right now. Parker finished up with his last students about fifteen minutes ago."

"I'll go give them a hand," Allie said. "I can hardly wait to hear their big news."

Samantha grinned. "You'll be thrilled," she said.

"No hints?" Allie asked teasingly.

Samantha shook her head. "You'll just have to wait," she said, turning back to Melody and Orion.

When Allie peered through the doors to the indoor arena, she saw that the space was empty. The jumps from the lesson had been stored against one wall, and the footing had been raked smooth.

She headed for the stalls, stopping at Samantha's office to peek at the sleeping twins. Kaitlin looked up from the filing cabinet and gave a small wave, then touched her finger to her lips and pointed at a cot against one wall. Luke and Leah were sleeping on the low bed, each of them curled up on one end of it. Their sweet, contented expressions made Allie smile. "They're so adorable," she whispered.

Kaitlin rolled her eyes. "When they're sleeping," she said in a low voice. "When they're awake, they hardly stand still long enough to be adorable."

Allie stifled a laugh, then hurried away before she woke the children. She walked down the long aisle of the barn, pausing at an occasional stall to visit Tor and

Samantha's hunters, ending at Finn McCoul's stall. The big stallion, the foundation horse for Whisperwood's breeding program, snorted softly when she walked by his stall, and she stopped to give the tall brown horse a pat on the nose. "You're such a handsome guy," she said, stroking the hollow under his throat. Finn bobbed his head contentedly, letting Allie pet him. "Enough," she finally said. "But next time I come, I'll remember an apple for you."

She walked out of the end door and around to the paddocks behind the barn. Sterling Dream, the big gray mare that Christina had sold to Whisperwood when she had started racing Wonder's Star, was dozing in the thin fall sunlight, one hip cocked to the side, her head drooping. Sterling's sides were getting round with the foal she was expecting in the early spring. Parker and Christina stood shoulder to shoulder at the fence, gazing at the mare.

"How's she doing?" Allie asked when she stopped beside them, her eyes on the dozing mare.

"She seems pretty content," Christina said, smiling at Allie. "I think she's going to be a great dam."

Parker nodded. "It'll be interesting to see if this foal is a flat-track racer or a jumper."

"I'm predicting the flat," Christina said. "Sterling's bloodlines all leaned toward racing. She was just a renegade."

Parker chuckled. "Like you?"

Christina wrinkled her nose at him. "I had to make up my own mind about racing, just like Sterling made up her mind that she was a jumper."

When Christina was twelve, her parents had given her their interest in Legacy, hoping that owning her own racehorse would encourage her interest in racing. But Christina had been determined to compete in eventing and had never connected with Legacy. When she'd seen Sterling at the racetrack, fighting her jockey and eagerly jumping obstacles not meant to be jumped, Christina had known the mare was meant to be hers. With her parents' reluctant permission, she had traded her interest in Wonder's Legacy for Sterling.

Shortly afterward Ashleigh had made the decision to breed Ashleigh's Wonder one more time. Unfortunately, having the foal had cost Wonder her life. But Christina had bonded closely with the sickly orphan and gave up eventing to pursue a career as a jockey. After an impressive career on the track, Wonder's Star had retired from racing the previous year and was now standing stud at Whitebrook, while Christina was working toward her college degree in veterinary medicine.

Sterling woke from her nap and raised her head, nickering softly at the trio standing at the fence. Allie slipped between two of the rails and crossed the paddock.

"Look at you," she crooned, running a hand along Sterling's flank. "You're going to be such a great mom. I can hardly wait to see what Legacy's and your foal looks like." She petted Sterling's sleek neck. "Do you think it's going to be more interested in racing or jumping?"

Sterling looked indifferent, and Allie laughed. "I know, I know. You just want a strong, healthy foal, right? Typical mother." She pressed her hand to Sterling's side, wishing she could feel the foal move, but it would be several more weeks before that would happen.

She left the mare and crossed the paddock to eye Christina and Parker. "Do I get the news now?" she asked.

"In a few minutes," Christina said. "We need to go back to the barn first."

"Fine," Allie said, rolling her eyes. "I just want to know what all the mystery is."

"You'll know soon," Parker said with a grin.

When they returned to the barn, Samantha met them in the aisle, flanked by Luke and Leah, who had awakened in the meantime. When the twins saw Allie, they broke away from their mother and moved as fast as their little legs could carry them, their arms outstretched.

Laughing, Allie dropped to her knees and opened her arms, letting out an exaggerated "oof" when the toddlers flung themselves at her.

"My two favorite FEWs," she said, hugging the children.

"FEWs?" Christina asked, reaching down to sweep a giggling Leah into her arms.

"Future Equestrians of Whisperwood," Allie explained, holding Luke up to Parker. Parker swung the little boy onto his shoulder and continued down the aisle with a bouncing gait, much to Luke's delight.

"Maureen O'Brien from the *Herald* should be here any minute," Samantha said to Parker. "Are you ready to make your big announcement?" She held her arms out for Luke, but he clung to Parker, shaking his head.

"No, no, no," he told his mother, patting Parker's dark hair.

"He's fine," Parker said with a grin. "I can hold my best little buddy while I talk to the press."

"What's someone from the paper doing here?" Allie asked. "Is your news so big that you have to have an interview with a reporter?" She knew that engagement announcements were usually just sent in to the paper, but then, with so many years of feuding over control of Wonder's foals and competing on the track, the rivalry between Townsend Acres and Whitebrook was well known. The engagement of the heir to Townsend Acres to Mike and Ashleigh's only child would be huge news in the racing world.

Increasingly curious, Allie joined the others as they walked back through the barn. When they got close to Samantha's office, Allie saw a slender woman in a dark suit waiting by the door. She had a notebook and tape recorder in her hands and was talking to Kaitlin, who was standing in the doorway.

"Maureen!" Samantha called.

The woman looked over, a smile brightening her

face. "Hi, Sammy," she said, then turned back to Kaitlin. "Thanks for the information. It'll go well in the piece I'm writing."

Samantha quickly introduced Maureen to Allie. "Even in high school, Maureen was a great journalist," she said. "After we graduated, she majored in journalism at the University of Kentucky, then went to work for the *Lexington Herald*."

"And all these years later, I'm still there," Maureen said. "I do more editing than writing now, but this was one story I wanted to do myself."

"Do you want to sit down in my office?" Samantha asked.

"Actually, I'd like to go see Parker's horses, if that's all right."

Allie looked from Maureen to Parker, more puzzled than ever. Apparently the announcement had nothing to do with Christina, and although she was a little disappointed, Allie was still aching to hear what it was.

"Right this way," Parker said, gesturing for the reporter to follow him He led the way through the barn to where his horses, Wizard of Oz, Black Hawke, and Foxglove, were in their stalls. With Luke still clinging to his neck, Parker leaned against Foxy's stall. The big bay mare reached her nose over the stall, and Luke leaned over Parker's shoulder to rub the white star between her eyes.

"Foxy," he said. The mare pressed her head forward, clearly enjoying the attention. The two younger horses, both geldings, hung their heads over their stall doors, eyeing the people gathered in front of the stalls.

Maureen turned on her tape recorder and flipped open her notebook, glancing at the list of questions she had for Parker. Allie stood nearby, waiting impatiently.

"Let's start at the beginning," Maureen said to Parker. "Tell me how you got started with horses. You grew up at Townsend Acres, surrounded by racehorses, right?"

"Nope," Parker said with a slight grimace. "I went to school in England. I wasn't around Townsend Acres much until I was a teenager. And I never cared about racing. All I ever wanted to do was combined training."

"And you've excelled," Maureen noted. "Your parents must be thrilled by your accomplishments."

Parker pinched his lips together. "Not exactly," he finally said. "They would have preferred it if I had been more interested in the family business."

"Parker's very independent," Christina interjected.

"He's very competitive and focused." A tiny smile played on her lips. "A lot like his father."

Allie glanced from Christina to Parker, seeing Parker's eyes narrow a little. She knew that Brad and Lavinia had done little to support Parker's passion for jumping, and she knew that Christina's comparing him to Brad had to make him mad.

But Parker just rolled his eyes. Apparently he and Christina had covered this subject before.

Maureen was nodding in understanding. "It's tough for people with strong personalities to grow up with parents who are the same way." She smiled at Parker. "I take it you don't want the article to dwell much on Townsend Acres."

Parker finally relaxed a little. "That would be good," he said. "My successes in three-day eventing have very little to do with my family owning some racehorses."

"But you can't ignore the fact that you're a Townsend," Christina said. "Everyone in Kentucky knows at least a little about your family."

"I'd rather have the focus be on Whisperwood," Parker said, looking at Samantha. "Townsend Acres doesn't need any more publicity. Thanks to Sammy and Tor, I've been able to pursue my dream and earn a living by teaching what I know best."

"I'll be sure to make Samantha's place an important feature," Maureen promised. "And I'll touch lightly on Townsend Acres. Obviously you're not happy with your folks, but we don't need to offend them."

"To tell you the truth, I really don't care if you don't mention them at all," Parker said.

Christina put a hand on Parker's arm. "So talk about how much your grandfather has done for you," she said, then pointed at Black Hawke. "That way you're giving credit to the Townsends without saying much about your father."

Parker gazed at Christina. "You're right," he said, then turned to Maureen. "My grandfather, Clay Townsend, has done a lot to help me." He reached over to stroke Black Hawke's gleaming neck. "He gave this guy to me. Foxy here is getting a little too old to stand up to the rigors of competition, so I use her for backup. She's extremely talented, but I don't want to push her." He smiled. "Without a string of world-class jumpers, I'd never have gotten this close to achieving my dream."

"And what was that dream?" Maureen inquired,

leaning forward as she waited for Parker to answer the question.

Parker looked at Samantha, his eyes sparkling. "My dream has always been to compete in the Olympics," he said. "And yesterday I got a notice from the team captain that I'm on the United States Olympic equestrian team."

Allie gaped at Parker. "You're serious?"

Parker nodded, standing a little straighter as his smile grew even wider. "Dead serious," he said. "With the help and support of some great people, and with some outstanding horses, I'm going for the gold!"

3

ALLIE STARED AT PARKER AS THE NEWS SANK IN. "THE Olympics?" she repeated, feeling her jaw drop. "You're on the team?"

Parker grinned at her. "*We're* on the team," he said, nodding toward his horses. "Ozzie, Black Hawke, Foxy, and me. Don't sound so shocked." He made a face at her. "I think we'll do okay."

"You'll do more than okay!" Allie exclaimed, feeling her cheeks grow hot. "I know you're the best rider on the team. I didn't mean it to sound like I was surprised. I'm just, uh . . ." She gave him an embarrassed smile. "Surprised, I guess."

Parker burst into laughter and reached over to give Allie's shoulder a light squeeze. "I know," he said. "The truth is, when Captain Donnelly called me, I said the same thing: 'I'm on the team?' "

Maureen looked at Christina and smiled. "As a well-known success in racing, you know what kind of work it takes to get to the top. You must be elated for Parker."

Christina smiled at Parker. "Parker's overcome a lot more than I ever had to," she said. "He really has done it on his own." She patted her boyfriend's arm. "I've been lucky enough to have the support of my entire family all along to get where I am as a jockey. Parker's worked hard to prove himself, and he's made it against the odds. I'm incredibly proud of what he's accomplished."

"I have to give credit to some fantastic coaches, too," Parker said. "I've gotten a lot of help from great people like Sammy and Tor." He looked at Samantha and smiled fondly. "People who believed in me."

"Don't forget Jack Dalton," Samantha said. "All that time in England paid off, too."

Parker nodded. "Jack is the toughest instructor I've ever met," he said. "His training helped me take my riding to where it is now, world-class level. I do owe him a lot."

Maureen shut off the recorder and closed her notebook. "This is going to make great copy," she said. "I can hardly wait to write the story." She glanced at Parker. "I'll be careful how I include your family," she said. "Off the record, I do remember the rough times Sammy and Ashleigh went through with your dad when Wonder's Pride was racing."

"Ugh," Samantha said. "I don't even like to think about that." She shook her head. "I still have bad memories of the way he pushed Pride to the point of exhaustion."

Christina shrugged. "Brad likes to win, no matter what the cost," she said.

"He sure isn't a graceful loser," Parker added.

Maureen gave Parker an understanding smile. "Your father is a pretty strong-willed person to stand up to. Are you sure you want to exclude him from the article? It could make for some even harder feelings between you two."

Parker wrinkled his nose. "I'm not worried about hurting his feelings," he said. "But you can write the article however you want. Just make sure you promote

Whisperwood. It could be good for business around here, and if I can pay Tor and Sammy back a little for all their help, that would be great."

"Got it," Maureen said. She turned to Samantha. "You said you had some photos of Parker in the office. Can we go through those so I can pick some for the paper?"

Samantha and Maureen walked away, and Allie moved closer to Parker and Christina. "The Olympics," she said again, still surprised by the announcement. "I thought you were going to say you two were getting engaged."

Christina laughed. "Not yet," she said, looking at Parker. "I still have to finish school, and Parker has the Olympics to focus on now. Maybe in a couple of years that'll be the next big news we have to share."

Allie reached over the stall wall to stroke Foxy's neck. "You're going to do great," she told the muscular mare. "You'll make the cross-country course look like a Sunday hack." She sighed. "I do miss having the time to jump just for fun."

"Do you remember the time you tried to jump Legacy?" Parker asked Christina.

"Oh, don't bring that up." Christina groaned, burying her face in Leah's red locks.

The little girl giggled and wriggled in Christina's arms. "Down," she demanded. "Teabiscuit."

Allie smiled. The twins' dapple gray Shetland pony was the friendliest little horse she had ever met, and Luke and Leah adored him.

"Teabiscuit!" Luke exclaimed, squirming in Parker's arms.

Kaitlin came up the aisle and grinned at Parker. "Congratulations," she said. "I knew you could do it."

"Thanks," Parker said.

"Teabiscuit now," Leah insisted.

"I'll take them," Kaitlin offered, holding her arms out to take Luke from Parker.

"I thought you liked them better when they were sleeping," Allie teased the other girl.

Kaitlin shook her head. "I like them all the time," she admitted. "They just have a lot of energy."

Christina and Tor set the twins down, and they grabbed Kaitlin's hands.

"Let's go see your pony," she said, leading them down the barn to Teabiscuit's stall.

"What happened when you jumped Legacy?" Allie asked, looking from Parker to Christina. "Did he refuse?"

"Not exactly," Christina replied, her face turning

pink as she thought back. "Mom and Dad were pretty reluctant to let me exercise-ride, even though they were both really encouraging me to be a jockey. I wanted to prove to them that I could be Legacy's exercise rider. I didn't see much point in owning a horse I couldn't even ride. So I sneaked out with Legacy one morning. I really did plan to take him onto the track. But then I spotted a fallen tree . . ." Her voice trailed off.

"You should have known Chris then," Parker said. "Anything on the ground was a potential jump, and she was completely fearless." He shook his head. "She just didn't think that one through all the way."

"Hey," Christina exclaimed, "I was only twelve!"

Allie couldn't imagine Legacy sailing over a jump, but the idea intrigued her. "Did he clear the jump?" she asked.

"Well," Christina said slowly, "he ran away with me first, and he was pretty confused about being off the training oval. When we reached the tree he was going too fast to stop. It was actually a great jump. But when I tried to jump him a second time, he wasn't very comfortable with it."

"With proper training, I think Legacy could do

some cross-country," Parker said. "He just wasn't mentally prepared to go hopping over a fallen tree."

"It didn't matter," Christina said. "After that, I'd never have tried it with him again."

"Why not?" Allie asked.

"Because he just didn't feel right to me," Christina explained. "I wanted a horse that was passionate about jumping, which is where Sterling fit in perfectly. Besides, Legacy was barely two, and you know how delicate a young Thoroughbred's legs are."

Allie stared at her, amazed that Christina would have been so reckless with a horse. "That wasn't such a good idea," she said, shaking her head. Jumping a horse while it was too young could cause permanent damage, and a horse with great potential would be useless, nothing more than what horse people referred to as a "pasture ornament."

"I didn't always use the best judgment in the world," Christina said, making a face. "I was pretty self-centered back then. It wasn't until I had Star to take care of that I started to do some growing up."

Parker reached over to rest his hand on hers. "But everything worked out," he said. "You're an amazingly talented jockey, you've made a great name for yourself on the track, and you've made lots of other good decisions since you were younger." He looked at Allie and wiggled his eyebrows. "The best decision she made was to start dating me."

Christina shot him a bright smile. "That *was* a good decision, wasn't it?" she agreed, then turned back to Allie. "Not only was trying to jump Legacy not the best idea I ever had," she said, "but Mom caught me."

"And you got banned from riding him ever again?"

"Oh, no," Christina said. "I ended up being his exercise rider. Mom understood about my wanting to feel like he was my horse, and he did really well in training. But I still wanted to be an event rider, and Legacy was better suited to the flat track."

Allie gazed at Christina thoughtfully. "I love racing," she said. "But I'd still like to do some cross-country."

Christina nodded. "Now that Legacy's a mature horse, you might want to see how he does on the jumps."

"And his bloodlines include stallions who've sired great eventing horses." Parker smiled at Allie.

Allie raised her eyebrows. "I never thought to ask before," she said, "but one of you would probably know. Who picked Gold Legacy as his sire?"

Parker and Christina both made faces.

"That was my dad," Parker said. "He wanted a foal out of Wonder with some strong ties to the Darley Arabian line. I know he was upset that my grandfather had let Champion go, and he wanted a stud colt that would improve Wonder's progeny. He was thinking ahead to Townsend Acres' breeding program."

"My mom and Parker's dad fought for a long time over what stallion to use," Christina said. "It seemed like there was a battle every time breeding season rolled around after Parker's grandfather, Clay, turned Townsend Acres over to Brad. Then there were some long, nasty phone calls and meetings between my parents and Brad. But when Brad got a chance to use Gold Legacy, Mom was all for breeding Wonder to a line-bred Nasrullah great-grandson."

"I've always thought of the Nasrullah line as dynamite racehorses, not eventers," Allie said. "Gold Legacy's sire, Mr. Prospector, sired great racehorses."

Parker grinned. "Then you'd better read up a little more on Legacy's relatives," he said. "There are a lot of the Darley Arabian descendants competing in combined training. Besides," he continued, "every horse can jump. You know that. It's just that some are better at it than others, and some just don't have the mind for it. If you want to bring Legacy over here while I'm around, we could try him out in the arena."

"That would be great," Allie said enthusiastically. With Parker to help her, maybe she could take Legacy over a few jumps and learn a bit from an Olympic-class rider. Not that she was ever going to compete in eventing, but she still enjoyed popping over a fence on occasion.

She drove home, eager to share the exciting news of Parker's appointment to the Olympic team with Cindy, and ask about trailering Legacy to Whisperwood for a jumping lesson.

When she arrived at Tall Oaks, she parked at the barn and hurried inside. She hadn't meant to stay so long at Whisperwood, and she had chores to do as well as her homework. Elizabeth met her just inside the barn door. "You're to go up to the house," the groom said, looking serious.

"But I have work to do first," Allie protested. "It isn't that late."

Elizabeth shook her head firmly. "Not this afternoon," she said, the twinkle in her eyes hinting that something good was waiting for Allie, even though she was working hard at keeping a stern expression on her face. "Those were Ben and Cindy's orders, and if you don't get up to the house, you'll get me in trouble with both of my bosses. You don't want to do that, do you?"

"All right," Allie said slowly. She wanted to go see Legacy before she went up to the house, but instead she left the barn. As she drove past the caretaker's cottage where she and Cindy had lived until the previous spring, she gazed fondly at the small house. It had been her first home in Kentucky, and she had good memories of living there.

When Ben and Cindy had gotten married, Cindy and Allie had moved into the grand house on the hill. Now Allie had her own suite of rooms, with magnificent views from every window. She still felt as though she should pinch herself awake whenever she walked through the massive house.

"I'm home," she called when she entered the spacious foyer. She still wasn't quite used to the way her voice echoed in the high-ceilinged room. No one answered, and she crossed the marble floor, setting her schoolbooks on a side table that she had been told was as old as the Civil War–era mansion. She peeked into

Ben's office, the first room off the foyer, but it was empty, and she strode through the arched doorway that led to the sitting room. There was a fire crackling on the flagstone hearth, but no one was sitting in any of the overstuffed leather chairs that flanked the large fireplace. She hurried into the dining room and stopped.

The table had been set for three, complete with Tall Oaks' best china, the heavy silver flatware that was used for special occasions, and crystal water goblets, a thin slice of lemon floating in each glass. Glass-chimneyed lamps sent soft golden light across the table. Allie looked around curiously, trying to figure out what was going on. There weren't any birthdays to celebrate, it wasn't Ben and Cindy's anniversary, and no extra places were set, so there obviously weren't any visitors for dinner.

"There you are!" Cindy came in from the kitchen. Allie's foster mother was wearing a pair of dark slacks and a white Aran sweater, her short blond hair tucked behind her ears. She set a covered serving platter on the table, and Allie noticed the sparkle of the large diamond on her left hand.

Ben and Cindy's wedding had been a grand show.

They'd gotten married on the lawn in front of the mansion, with a huge crowd in attendance. Ben's parents had flown over from Dubai for the wedding. Mr. al-Rihani had seemed gruff, but when a rare smile crossed his face, Allie could see how much Ben looked like him. She had taken an immediate liking to Ben's mother, who had insisted that Allie call her Zahra. She had started calling Allie Ala, too, and treated her like a beloved granddaughter from the very first time they met.

"You must come to Dubai," Zahra told her, and Allie had promised she would, thinking someday she would ride a Tall Oaks Thoroughbred in the Dubai Cup, the way Cindy had ridden Champion in the great race. After a tough duel with a Thoroughbred called Limitless Time, Cindy and Champion had won the race by a length. Allie imagined herself galloping across the desert sand, then smiled. It wasn't something she'd ever dreamed of before coming to Tall Oaks, but now her life seemed full of possibilities.

She looked at the perfectly set table and at Cindy, dressed so nicely, and gave her foster mother a piercing look. "What's going on?" she asked. "Are we having company tonight?"

Cindy shook her head. "You'll find out soon enough," she said.

Allie didn't know if she wanted to laugh or yell. "I've been hearing that all afternoon," she said, shaking her head. "Has Lexington become the land of testing Allie's patience?"

"Go wash up," Cindy said instead of answering Allie's question. Her eyes were twinkling when she looked at Allie. "You'll find out as soon as you and Ben are at the table. It's pretty big news, and waiting a few more minutes won't kill you."

What more big news could there be today? Allie wondered as she walked through the house. She picked up her schoolbooks and carried them to her room, then quickly washed up and returned to the dining room. Ben and Cindy were seated at the table, waiting for her.

"Good evening," Ben said, rising as Allie approached the table. She smiled to herself. She was getting used to the polite manners that living in the grand mansion seemed to demand. Life had changed so much since she'd moved to Kentucky, and every day felt like a new adventure.

"Dinner smells yummy," she said, settling onto her chair.

"Luis left a casserole for us," Cindy said. "All I had to do was heat it up."

Ben laughed. "He knows your cooking skills," he told Cindy, leaning over to pat her arm.

Allie looked up to see Ben and Cindy watching her expectantly. "You're both up to something," Allie said, narrowing her eyes at them. "When are you going to tell me what this is about?"

"Don't forget to put your napkin on your lap," Cindy said.

Allie stifled a laugh. When she and Cindy had lived in the cottage they had usually heated frozen entrees in the microwave oven and used paper towels instead of the fine linens that graced the mansion's oak dining table. But she picked up her napkin agreeably, and saw an envelope that had been hidden beneath it.

"What's this?" she asked, picking it up. The envelope had been addressed to Ben and Cindy al-Rihani, and the return address was for the social services office that had overseen Cindy's being Allie's foster mother.

After the wedding, Ben and Cindy had petitioned to adopt Allie, but for months there had been no word as to whether the adoption would be approved or not. It had seemed like such a simple thing, but for some reason the court system made it cumbersome and complicated.

"Open it," Ben said, leaning forward, his dark eyes shining.

With trembling hands, Allie tore the envelope open and pulled out a sheaf of formal-looking papers. She started to read the complex wording, searching for the one word that would make sense of everything. Finally, near the end of the third page, she found it: *approved*. Her adoption had been approved. She looked up at Ben and Cindy, the papers clutched to her chest. "I'm yours!" she exclaimed.

Ben and Cindy beamed and Allie felt warmed by their smiles.

"We're a real family," Cindy announced. "It's official, and nothing can change that." She gazed at Allie warmly. "You're our daughter, Allison, now and forever."

4

DINNER PASSED IN A BLUR FOR ALLIE. TOO WOUND UP TO eat, she tried to take some bites of the wonderful food Luis had left for them, but she could barely taste it. Still, it was a good kind of wound-up feeling. She had waited so long for this, and wanted so badly for the adoption to come through, to be part of a real family again. But now that it was official, it seemed almost like a dream.

"Are you all right?" Cindy asked, frowning slightly.

Allie nodded, tucking another bite of casserole into her mouth. "Fine," she said. "I guess I'm just not very hungry tonight. May I be excused?"

"Of course," Ben said with a smile.

Allie picked up her dishes and carried them to the kitchen, then went to her room to call Lila to share the news.

"That's the most excellent thing I've heard all day," Lila said enthusiastically. "I think this calls for another party, don't you?"

Allie chuckled. "Maybe later," she said. "Right now I'm still getting used to the feeling of being someone's kid again."

"I'll see you tomorrow at school," Lila said. "I need to figure out what kind of present you give someone who's just been adopted."

At that Allie laughed. "I got the best present of all already," she told her friend. "I have two of the greatest people I know as my parents, and I have you for a best friend."

After she got off the phone, Allie grabbed a jacket and went back to the kitchen. Since it was Luis's day off, the big room was quiet. When Allie had first moved into the mansion, Luis had invited her into the kitchen.

"You should know," he said, narrowing his eyes in an attempt to look forbidding, "that no one enters my domain without my express permission." He waved his hand dramatically. "I am ferocious about protecting my kitchen." Then his round face broke into a smile. "But you, Allison, are welcome here anytime." Then he had informed her that he would keep a stock of horse food in one bin in the big stainless-steel refrigerator, and he had done just that. Sometimes there were apples, sometimes carrots, and on occasion she found muffins in the bin, labeled "horse muffins from an old family recipe." When she had asked about it, Luis had admitted that he'd found the recipe in a horse magazine and had baked them especially for Legacy.

This evening she pulled a few carrots from a bag and stuffed them into her jacket pocket, then headed back down to the barn. The stable was quiet, the only sounds those of the horses in their stalls, still crunching on their hay. Most of the lights were off, but every third bulb was burning, keeping the aisles lit well enough to see clearly. Allie strolled past the stalls, pausing to give Alpine Meadow a little attention. The chestnut filly nuzzled Allie's hand, not as interested in a piece of carrot as she was in being petted. Allie's next stop was at Charming Miss's stall. The tall bay filly took the bit of carrot Allie held out for her and chewed it eagerly, then shoved her nose at Allie's hand, looking for more.

"That's all you get," Allie said, stroking the racehorse's sleek, mahogany-colored nose. Further into the barn, she stopped to visit Perfect Image. The big black mare swiveled her ears, starting to pin them, until she caught Allie's scent. Then a low nicker rumbled in her throat, and Allie leaned over the wall to pat Image's glossy neck. "How's my cranky old girl?" she asked.

Image had been born at Tall Oaks, but when the previous owner had run into financial problems, she had sold the young Thoroughbred to Melanie's father, Will Graham, and a rock musician, Jazz Taylor. Melanie had trained and raced Image, winning the Kentucky Derby with the well-bred racehorse. But Image had broken her leg at the finish line, abruptly ending her racing career. Ben and Cindy had bought the mare, who was now in foal to Wonder's Champion. Everyone at Tall Oaks was eager to see what kind of foal she would drop.

"Is it going to be chestnut or black?" Allie asked the mare, who nuzzled at her hand, searching for a tidbit. "I hope you have a black filly who looks just like you." She rubbed Image's neck, then fed her a piece of carrot.

After leaving Image, Allie paused at some of the other mares' stalls. Since coming to Tall Oaks, she had seen the once-empty barns fill with Thoroughbreds, some of them talented racehorses, some broodmares with excellent bloodlines that Ben and Cindy planned to use to produce their own exceptional foal crops.

In the stallion barn, she stopped to visit Champion. The chestnut stallion, born at Whitebrook, had been sold to Ben's father and had spent several years in the United Arab Emirates before returning to the United States. Champion had sired several world-class colts and fillies and was now the foundation sire for Tall Oaks' breeding program.

Khan, the chestnut stallion that had been included in the sale when Ben bought Tall Oaks, was still eating his dinner when Allie passed him. She offered him a bite of carrot, but the stallion ignored her as he tore another mouthful of hay from the net hanging in one corner of his stall.

Next to Khan was Hi Jinx, Melanie's little chestnut stallion. Although the horse had some talent, Melanie had struggled to turn him into a successful racehorse.

Jinx had won enough races to command a reasonable stud fee, and in exchange for his board at Tall Oaks, Melanie raced for the farm on occasion. Although he was difficult and unpredictable, Allie liked the horse, who popped his head up when she walked up, perking his ears and pressing his nose into her hand, inhaling deeply.

"How's old Jinxy doing?" Allie asked affectionately, rubbing the Thoroughbred's poll while she fished another piece of carrot from her pocket. "Have you been a good boy today?"

Jinx snorted, using his lips to snag the treat from her palm.

"I'll take that as a maybe," she said with a smile, then moved on down the aisle, stopping in front of Champion's Ghalib. The four-year-old chestnut looked like his sire, but he had his dam's body type. Bred in the United Arab Emirates, Ghalib had proven himself on the track, winning several stakes races as a three- and four-year-old. Cindy still had races planned for him during the Keeneland fall meet, and Allie was looking forward to riding the talented racehorse.

Finally, she walked on to where Legacy was nosing

around the floor of his stall, looking for any bits of grain or hay he might have missed.

"How's my big guy?" Allie asked, opening the stall door. Legacy raised his head and gazed at her as she let herself into his stall.

"You're such a sweetie," she murmured, wrapping her arms around the stallion's neck. "I have some great news—maybe not as huge as Parker's getting to ride in the Olympics, but pretty big news for me." As she fed him bits of carrot, Allie told him about the adoption. "I just don't know about changing my last name," she said. "I'll always be Allie Avery, but I don't want to hurt Ben and Cindy's feelings. How do you think Allie al-Rihani sounds?"

"Rather exotic," a voice behind her said.

Allie turned to see Ben in the aisle.

"When you disappeared after dinner we didn't have to think hard to figure out where you'd gone," Ben said, reaching into the stall to pet Legacy. "And to set your worries to rest, you don't have to change your name unless you choose to. Cindy and I do understand."

Allie smiled at her father. "Thanks," she said. "I just hadn't thought much about it until now. Is it okay if I take my time deciding?"

"Of course," Ben said. "I know we've been waiting a long while for this to really happen, but it still must be pretty overwhelming for you."

Allie offered him a crooked smile. "It is," she admitted. "I still miss my . . . my . . ." She fumbled for the right words. Ben and Cindy were legally her parents now.

"Your mom and dad," Ben said, nodding. "We aren't replacements for Craig and Jilly, Allie. You know that. I want you to know I'd be honored if you took al-Rihani as a last name, but Avery is a fine name as well. No matter what you choose, Ala, I'll always think of you as my daughter."

Allie felt tears well up in her eyes as she thought of her parents, gone for over two years now. Even with the passing of so much time, memories of them arose every day. And even though the horrible ache had faded over time, thinking of them still hurt. She turned to look at Legacy, not wanting Ben to see her cry.

"Cindy is in her office going through some papers," Ben said. "Even though she has a barn manager now, she still seems to find a lot to do down here. I'm going to check on her." He started to walk away, then stopped. "Come and get us before you leave, and we can walk back up to the house together."

Allie listened as his footsteps faded as he walked off, leaving her with Legacy. She wrapped her arms around his muscled neck, burying her face in his sweet-smelling coat. "Mom and Dad would be so happy that things have worked out this way for me," she said. "I know they would."

Legacy pressed his jaw down on her shoulder in a horsy hug, and Allie stroked his neck. Slowly the urge to cry faded, and she stepped back to look at the big chestnut stallion, remembering Parker's offer. "There's one other thing, boy. How do you feel about trying a few jumps at Whisperwood?"

Legacy sniffed at her hand, searching for more carrot, and she fed him a chunk.

"It wouldn't be like when you were a two-year-old and went on a wild ride with Christina," Allie reassured him. "I think you might like it. We could take it easy, so you won't be surprised by any of the jumps."

She left the horse a few minutes later and walked to Cindy's office. The lights were on, and she heard Ben and Cindy talking about some upcoming races, and scheduling for the winter meets in Florida. A contented smile settled on Allie's face, and she strolled into the room.

"Would it be all right if I took Legacy over to Whisperwood to try jumping him?" she asked, looking from Ben to Cindy. "Parker offered to help me, and it sounded like fun."

Ben nodded toward Cindy. "We may be husband and wife," he said, "but Cindy will always be the boss in the barn. It's entirely up to her."

"Do you miss eventing?" Cindy asked.

"A little," Allie admitted. "But more than that, I think it would be fun to see what Legacy can do."

"Having fun is important," Cindy agreed. "I'm fine with it." Then she leaned forward, resting her elbows on her desk. "Speaking of Parker, what was the big mystery announcement from Whisperwood?"

"I completely forgot to tell you!" Allie exclaimed, clapping her hands together. "Parker's going to the Olympics!"

A grin spread across Cindy's face, and Ben nodded with approval.

"That's wonderful," Cindy said, leaning back. "Parker's worked hard to get a spot on the team, and he deserves it."

"Samantha's friend from high school, Maureen O'Brien, came to do an interview. Parker didn't want her even to mention Townsend Acres in the article she's writing. But Christina got him to see that it would be better for him to at least acknowledge his family's farm."

Cindy wrinkled her nose and nodded. "I know how he feels," she said. "When I first came to Whitebrook and the Townsends co-owned Wonder and all her foals, Brad and Lavinia made things pretty miserable for everyone at Whitebrook, and Lavinia seemed to go out of her way to make things rough for me." She shook her head, as though to rid it of negative thoughts of Lavinia. "When Ian and Beth were fighting with Children's Services to adopt me, Lavinia did her best to keep it from happening."

"Why would she do that?" Allie asked, puzzled. She knew Parker's mother was stuffy and rude, but to do something that hurtful to someone else just didn't make sense.

"She thought I'd stolen a watch from her," Cindy said, grimacing.

"Well," Ben said, "you weren't exactly an angel back then."

"But I wasn't a thief," Cindy retorted.

"Really?" Ben asked, raising his eyebrows. "It

seems to me that was about the same time you had that stolen horse."

"You what?" Allie gaped at Cindy, shaking her head in disbelief. She plopped down on an empty chair and leaned forward, eyeing her mother expectantly. "I never heard about that."

Cindy raised her hands in the air and laughed. "Guilty with a reasonable explanation, of course," she said.

Allie narrowed her eyes and cocked her head. "So," she said slowly, "can I hang on to that bit of justification when I do something major that could get me into trouble? Guilty with an explanation?"

Ben burst into laughter. "I think she has something there, Cindy."

Cindy groaned, then made a face and nodded. "One time, and it had better be an explanation as good as mine," she replied, folding her arms in front of her as she looked at Allie.

"So tell me about your stolen horse." Allie rested her elbows on her knees.

"He was a beautiful gray two-year-old," Cindy said, a fond smile on her face. "He was being horribly abused, and when he got away from the people who had him, I found him and hid him in a shed at Whitebrook for several weeks. At the time I was still on shaky ground as far as foster care, and the Children's Services caseworker didn't think Whitebrook was a good place to raise a child."

Allie rolled her eyes. She knew that uninformed people thought the worst of racetrack life. It didn't help that most of the stories that went around focused on the gambling and greed, drug abuse and shady characters. But the people Allie had met who were involved in racing treated her like family. She couldn't change other people's narrow-minded views of racing by protesting to Ben and Cindy, so she kept her mouth shut, eager to hear the rest of Cindy's tale.

"It did help that I had saved Lavinia's life when a horse almost trampled her, right around the time she found out she was expecting Parker."

"What?" Allie shook her head to clear it. "You saved Lavinia's life when she was trying to ruin yours?"

Cindy shrugged. "She's just a silly woman with more ego than common sense," she said. "If I hadn't grabbed that horse she fell off of, Parker might not be here now, so everything works out, right? And it turned out that Lavinia's watch had fallen inside a tack box, so I was off the hook for that."

"Who cares about her watch?" Allie said impatiently. "Tell me about the stolen horse."

"Oh, that," Cindy said teasingly. "After I found him I heard that a great racehorse had been stolen from his legal owners. It didn't take long for me to realize that I was harboring that same Thoroughbred and I was able to return him to his rightful owners."

"What was his name?" Allie asked curiously, wondering if she'd ever heard of him.

Cindy grinned. "Not *was*," she said. "*Is*. He's March to Glory."

"The Whitebrook stallion?" Allie gasped.

Cindy nodded. "The very same," she said.

"Wow," Allie said. "He's an awesome horse, but hiding him could have meant you would be taken away from Ian and Beth."

Cindy nodded. "It was worth the risk," she said. "I couldn't just stand by and let him be abused, but I should have come clean about it sooner." With that, she rose and stretched, then looked at Ben. "Are you two ready to go back to the house? Luis left a tray of lemon tarts for dessert."

"Yummy," Allie said, standing up. The thought of the tarts made her mouth water, and suddenly the appetite she hadn't had for dinner came back with a vengeance. "We can have some tea, too, and you can tell me more about what it was like for you at Whitebrook when the Townsends had part ownership in the horses there."

Cindy shuddered. "It was pretty stressful," she said mildly. "Brad and Lavinia kept things on edge for a lot of years."

"I'm glad they don't have control of any of our horses," Allie said.

"Me too," Cindy said, then looked at her husband. "Thanks to you, Ben, Brad's been cut off from ever having a say in what we do with any of our horses related to Wonder."

Ben shrugged, shutting off the office light as they left the room. "I always enjoy outsmarting someone like Brad," he said easily. "And when I see how happy you are, it makes it doubly enjoyable."

"I never thought my life would turn out so perfectly," Cindy said, "but it has." She smiled at Ben, then hooked her arm in his as they walked out of the barn. "I have a wonderful husband, the best job in the world, and a great daughter. I think I'm the luckiest woman in the world."

"I feel like the luckiest girl in the world," Allie said. "You're both so good to me."

Ben draped his other arm over Allie's shoulders, pulling her close. "I think the three of us make a good team," he said, then looked at Cindy and smiled. "And I know without a doubt that I'm the luckiest man in the world."

5

THROUGH THE WINTER MONTHS, ALLIE MADE SEVERAL TRIPS to New York and Florida, racing for Tall Oaks, Whitebrook, and Celtic Meadows. She felt like an old pro walking into the terminal at the Keeneland Airport with her carry-on bag, greeting the familiar faces of the staff at the airport. Although the traveling was fun and the racing exciting, it was always good to come home and get back to her life in Kentucky, working at Tall Oaks and riding Legacy every chance she had.

Cindy sent Beckie down to Florida with both Charming Miss and Alpine Meadow to train for the winter meets at Calder and Gulfstream. When Allie flew to Gulfstream to race Charming in the six-furlong First Lady Handicap, she rode onto the track with all the confidence in the world that the filly would shine in the race, and she was right. It was a close, tense battle to the finish line, but in the end Charming put on her trademark burst of speed, nosing ahead of the lead horses to win the race.

The next day, Allie wasn't so sure her luck would hold out when she raced Alpine Meadow in the Banshee Breeze Stakes. Allie thought the mile-and-an-eighth race would be a challenge for Alpine, but when the filly broke from the gate ahead of the rest of the field, Allie had a feeling that the little chestnut wasn't going to let anyone catch her. When they crossed the finish line with a four-length gap between them and the second-place filly, Allie knew she was riding the greatest filly in racing.

"Just don't tell Image I said that," she murmured to Alpine as they posed in the winner's circle with Cindy and Beckie. "She's grouchy enough without being told she's only the second greatest."

Whitebrook sent Royal Blue down to run in the Grade III Mr. Prospector Handicap. Kevin brought the colt down for the farm, and Allie met him at the track.

"Where's Christina?" Allie asked when she saw Kevin at Royal Blue's stall.

Kevin looked around and raised his eyebrows. "You mean she isn't here?" he asked, feigning surprise.

"Cute, Kevin," Allie said, stroking the bay colt's elegant nose. "I thought she was going to ride him."

Kevin grinned at her. "Chris had a major test to take, and she, Ashleigh, and my dad agreed that you could do a great job for Whitebrook. If you want to race him, that is."

Allie gaped at Kevin. "Want to? You know I do. Besides," she added, "Mr. Prospector was Legacy's grandsire. I'll be racing for Whitebrook, and for Legacy and me."

When she mounted the bay colt the afternoon of the race, Allie knew that the competition was going to be the toughest she'd ever ridden against. Ten top-bred colts were circling the viewing ring, and she looked down at Kevin, forcing a grin. "I think we're going to need a ton of luck," she said as he led her toward the track.

"You'll be awesome out there," Kevin reassured her.

But when they broke from the gate, Royal Blue was in last place, and as they sped past each of the furlong markers, Allie's hopes that Whitebrook's next Triple Crown hopeful might at least place in the race faded fast. As they came out of the last curve and onto the straight stretch, however, the colt dug in and tore past the other horses, closing from last in a field of ten to score a two-and-a-half-length win.

As Allie slowed the colt, the roar of the crowd filled her ears, and she felt a rush of happiness. She was doing what she wanted to do most, and even better, she was succeeding at it.

She was quickly earning a reputation as a capable jockey, and her win on Royal Blue only solidified it. Soon she found herself with so many offers of horses to race that she had to turn down several of the trainers and owners who approached her.

In mid-January Cindy sent Ghalib to Aqueduct, where Allie rode him in the Aqueduct Handicap. Ghyllian Hollis had horses at the track for the meet, and Ghalib was kept in the Celtic Meadows stable.

Although Cindy wasn't able to be in New York for the race, Ben was there, standing at the owner's place in the viewing paddock when Terry Conley, one of Celtic Meadows' assistant trainers, brought Ghalib out for the race.

Allie stood beside Ben, watching the other horses in the field as they circled the paddock. She wasn't worried about Ghalib handling the distance, a mile and a sixteenth, but looking at the competition, she knew the race was going to be a challenge for both the racehorse and her.

At least four of the horses on the track that day had a lot of Nasrullah blood in them. "Seattle Supersonic," she said, watching a handsome chestnut horse prance past. "And there's Bold Attack, Sure Secret, and Bald Easy." Allie sucked in a deep breath. "This is going to be a tough race."

"Sounds like you're riding against the who's who of Thoroughbreds today," Ben commented, glancing down at her.

Allie fingered the chin strap of her helmet and met his eyes, giving him a nod. "We are," she said. "But Ghalib isn't quite a plow horse, either. We'll do fine."

"Just do your best and stay safe," Ben admonished her as Terry stopped the horse in front of the number four spot.

Allie rode onto the track, making note of the track condition. An early rain had softened the footing, but the Aqueduct track had been groomed smooth, and she was sure her mount wouldn't have a problem running.

When they were finally loaded in the gate, she leaned forward, bracing herself for the start. Ghalib charged onto the track when the gate sprang open, and Allie settled into position, sitting lightly over his shoulders, maneuvering the horse close to the inside rail. "We need to save all the track we can today," she told Ghalib, darting a quick look around to see how the field was playing out.

Ghalib was in a good position, close to the rail with only two horses in front of him. When Allie glanced to her right, she saw a big bay crowding up beside them, the jockey aiming his horse for a minute gap between the two lead horses.

"Hey!" she yelled, squeezing Ghalib onto the rail to avoid contact with the other horse. Ghalib checked himself and stumbled a little, sending Allie's heart thundering into her throat. She gave him his head and braced herself for a nasty spill, but Ghalib caught himself and tore along the track, trying to regain the ground they'd lost.

In the end, Bold Attack placed first, with Seattle Supersonic in second and Bald Easy in third. The big bay who had interfered with Ghalib had broken down near the end of the race, finishing last.

Fuming, Allie brought Ghalib to a jog, then turned him back to where Terry was coming onto the track to meet her.

"You don't need to file a protest," he told her as she jumped from Ghalib's back. "The officials already called it." He gave her a sympathetic smile as he took Ghalib's lead.

Allie walked with him toward the backside. Ben was waiting by the rail when they brought Ghalib off the track. He gave Allie a quick hug. "You did the right thing," he said. "You protected your horse and rode well. I couldn't be any prouder of you."

Still disappointed, not at losing the race but because they'd never know if Ghalib might have won under different circumstances, she smiled at her father. "Thanks," she said. "That makes me feel better."

Terry led Ghalib toward the barn, but Allie held back before going to the jockeys' lounge to change out of her silks. "I've been thinking . . ." she said to Ben.

He grinned. "That's good," he replied. "It means your brain is working just fine."

"Funny," Allie said, wrinkling her nose at him. "I

was thinking about what my mom and dad would say about changing my last name." She released a tiny sigh. "I know they'd tell me to follow my heart, and it keeps telling me to take al-Rihani as my last name. We're a family now, and I think my sharing the same last name makes it more real—for me, anyway."

"I'm pleased," Ben said, calmly but with a warm smile. "If this is what your heart wants, then so be it."

When she was home, Allie regularly took Legacy to Whisperwood, where she spent as much time as she could working with Parker. By the end of January, Legacy was proving himself to be a competent jumper, if not world-class.

"I told you he could jump," Parker said triumphantly when Allie finished a round of fences they had set up in the indoor arena. Legacy bobbed his head, and Allie petted his sleek neck. "He knew he could, too," she said, slipping from his back.

"Maybe now that things are warming up, we should go for a little cross-country ride," Parker suggested. "I think Legacy's ready for some new challenges, and time's getting short for me. Foxy, Black Hawke, Ozzie, and I have a busy spring coming up."

Allie eyed Legacy. "What do you think, fellow?" she asked. "Do you want to pop over some real fences and do some galloping in the open?"

"The weather looks good for Saturday," Parker said. "Do you want to go out for a few hours?"

"Of course!" Thanks to Parker's coaching, Allie's own skills at jumping had improved, and she looked forward to trying out a course that was a little more challenging than the jumps they set up in the arena.

While they were dismantling the equipment, Samantha came into the barn, followed by Luke and Leah. When the twins saw Parker and Allie, they left their mother and hurried across the arena.

"Up," Leah demanded, stopping in front of Allie, who lifted the little girl and propped her on her hip. Leah patted Legacy's nose. "Leah two," she informed the horse.

"Next week you'll be two," Parker told her, catching Luke under the arms and swinging him into the air.

Luke laughed, then leaned over to pet Legacy. "Ride?" he asked.

"Let me put Legacy up, then we'll get Teabiscuit out," Allie told the little boy.

"Are you going to be at their party?" Samantha asked Parker and Allie when she reached them.

"Wouldn't miss it for the world," Parker said.

Allie nodded, handing Leah to her mother. "Of course," she said. "Second birthdays are the best." She led Legacy away, and in a few minutes the horse was in an empty stall, tearing into a flake of hay Allie had given him. Allie quickly tacked the twins' chunky little pony and brought him back to the arena. For several minutes she and Parker led Luke and Leah around while Samantha watched.

After grooming the pony and putting him in his turnout, Allie went by Sterling's paddock to visit the mare. Her sides bulged, and as Allie ran her hand along the mare's glossy gray flank, she felt a lump roll under her hand. She gasped in delight. "I felt it move," she told Sterling, then laughed at herself. "You feel it all the time, don't you?"

Sterling exhaled, nudging at Allie's hand. "You'll be glad to have that baby running around beside you, won't you, girl?" she asked. "It has to be pretty uncomfortable for you." But Sterling seemed content, and soon Allie left her to relax in the late winter sun.

In the next turnout, Miss Battleship, Tor and Samantha's oldest broodmare, was standing with her head down, her eyes half closed. Like Sterling, her sides were full and round. *Pretty soon there'll be foals all over the place,* Allie thought. She was looking forward to the next several weeks, when the mares here and at Tall Oaks would be having their foals.

The morning of the twins' birthday party, Allie went to Whisperwood early. Parker was waiting for her at the barn. "Are you ready to do a little cross-country?" he asked, running a grooming brush down Foxy's red-brown flank.

"As soon as I get Legacy tacked up," Allie replied. "We can't be gone too long, because I promised Samantha I'd help her get the house ready for the birthday party."

"And I have work to do with the other horses before the party," Parker told her.

Soon they were both in the saddle, and Parker looked over at her. "Which direction shall we take?" he asked, gathering up Foxy's reins.

"I think the trails I used to take Sterling on would be good to start with," Allie said, adjusting her seat.

"It's been a long time since I did any cross-country riding, so I'd like to take a route that I know."

"Good idea," Parker agreed, squeezing Foxy's sides with his legs. He led them away from Whisperwood and into the outlying countryside, where several trails ran through the wooded acreage behind the farm.

Allie struggled to keep Legacy behind Foxy. "He doesn't want to follow," she told Parker. "He still has that racehorse mentality, and he wants to be the lead horse."

Parker chuckled, then shifted to the side of the narrow path so that Allie could bring Legacy up beside him. "It's a little close through here," he said.

"It widens out pretty soon," Allie reminded him, holding Legacy down to Foxy's steady pace. In a few minutes they turned onto a wider trail, and Legacy pushed to keep his nose ahead of Foxy's. The mare angled her head and pinned her ears slightly as Allie's Thoroughbred moved ahead of her.

"Foxy thinks Legacy needs a lesson in trail manners," Parker said, patting the mare's neck soothingly. The trail widened even more, and Parker eyed the smooth footing under the trees. "I think we can pick up the pace a bit," he said.

Allie urged Legacy into a canter, and for a few minutes they headed deeper into the trees. Then the trees thinned, ending in a large meadow. On the far side, Allie could see a wooden fence, one she had jumped several times on both Sterling and another Whisperwood mare, Irish Battleship. She slowed Legacy and looked over at Parker. "How's that look for his first outdoor jump?" she asked.

Parker nodded in approval. "Perfect," he said.

Allie brought Legacy back up to a collected canter, and they headed for the fence. Legacy pressed against the bit, trying to pick up speed, but Allie rated him carefully, gauging the distance to the jump. She rose into position and pressed her fists into Legacy's muscular neck, feeling the glorious rush of energy as Legacy took off and the incomparable sense of weightlessness as they sailed over the fence. Then Legacy's front hooves met the ground, and he gave a little buck as he landed.

Allie jolted onto his shoulders, then pushed herself back into the saddle and brought him to a stop. "What was that for?" she demanded, glad the horse's little stunt hadn't unseated her. She turned to see Foxy take the low fence smoothly, admiring Parker's perfect posture and the mare's expert moves as they gracefully cleared the obstacle.

Parker reined Foxy to a stop and grinned at Allie. "Legacy needs to work over a few more easy fences out here," he said. "I think he's just testing you."

Allie grimaced. "He almost outsmarted me," she said. "I wasn't expecting that little trick at the end. I'll be ready next time."

Parker nodded toward another fence. "Let's head over that one," he said. "Don't give him as much freedom with the reins, and bring your weight back as soon as his front legs are on solid ground."

For the next few minutes Allie took Legacy over the fences around the meadow, until after the fourth jump he quit misbehaving.

As she brought him to a stop, Parker applauded. "Good going," he said. "Now let's try some different jumps."

With Foxy in the lead, they cut across meadows, popping over some low fences and a few brush piles. As they rode, Allie forgot about the time and the twins' birthday. Legacy seemed to be gaining more confidence with every jump they cleared, and Parker led them to more challenging obstacles, even taking the horse over a fallen tree like the one Christina had jumped him over so many years ago.

"Time to go back," Parker announced finally.

Allie looked up at the sky, surprised to see how far the sun had traveled. "This was so great," she told Parker. "Thanks for taking the time to work with us."

"I was happy to do it," Parker said. "Foxy and I enjoyed ourselves." He jerked his chin toward an expanse of pastures. "There's a nice little brook over there," he said. "Did you ever jump it with Sterling?"

Allie shook her head. "I didn't realize it was there," she said. "We never went back to Whisperwood this way."

"It's a shortcut," Parker explained. "It'll take us half the time to get home if we go that route, but there are quite a few jumps along the way."

Confident in Legacy's jumping ability, and sure the horse could manage any of the jumps Parker led them to, she grinned and nodded.

"Then let's go!" Parker decided.

Allie urged Legacy into a canter, and as Parker and Foxy moved up beside them, she felt the horse lean into the bit, lengthening his strides. "You want to do a little real running, don't you, boy?" She put her weight a little more forward, letting him speed up.

"You want to make a steeplechase out of this, huh?" Parker called with a laugh. "We'll see you back at the barn." He shot her a quick look. "Just don't forget to stop him a good distance away from Whisperwood and walk him home."

"I know," Allie called back, then prepared herself for the first jump. Legacy sailed over the brush pile, and Allie steered him toward a fence, which he handled with ease. Parker and Foxy were cantering easily, and Parker took the mare over some jumps, going around others.

After a few more fences Allie could see the sunlight glinting on the water of the stream that meandered through the meadow.

Parker moved Foxy ahead of her, guiding them to the best place to jump the water, and Legacy yanked at the reins, not wanting the other horse in front of him. Allie fought him, trying to keep his speed controlled, but Legacy's race training was kicking in, and he struggled to get ahead of Parker and Foxy.

Allie watched Parker take his mount over the jump, and then the water was in front of them.

Legacy, focused on getting ahead in the race, was startled by the sun-sparkled water. Even as he started to jump, he twisted, trying to avoid the strange movement of the water beneath him. Instead of the perfect landing that Allie had anticipated, Legacy went into the water with a huge splash.

6

LEGACY WENT TO HIS KNEES, THEN SCRAMBLED TO GET BACK on his feet, struggling on the slippery streambed. Allie slid off the frightened horse's back, clinging to the reins.

"Easy, boy, easy," she said firmly, fighting to stay on her own feet while Legacy pulled against her. In his panic to get out of the water, he yanked hard against the hold she had on him. Already soaked up to her knees, Allie's feet shot out from under her. She fell into the chilly stream, gasping at the shock as the water soaked into her clothes.

Worried about Legacy getting loose and injuring

himself in a frantic run, she hung on to the reins as the horse lunged toward the bank. In order to get to her feet, she'd have to let him go, and Allie wasn't about to do that.

Parker jumped from Foxy's back and waded into the water far enough to take Legacy's reins from Allie. "I've got him," he said.

Allie released the reins, and Legacy charged up the bank. "You're all right," Parker said in a soothing voice, somehow managing to hold Foxy as well. The mare watched with mild interest, not reacting to Legacy's frantic, panicky dance, even when the distraught horse bumped into her.

Allie climbed up the bank, shivering. She was more miserable because of the failed jump than because she was cold and wet. Legacy was scooting in a nervous half circle around Parker, his eyes rolling and his nostrils flared.

Allie hurried over to Foxy, her soaked clothing pulling at her, her boots squelching with each step. As burdened as she was by her wet clothes, she let Parker handle Legacy, and she took Foxy's reins, moving the mare several feet away. "Is he hurt?" she asked anxiously.

Parker shook his head. "I don't think so," he said. "Just a little freaked out." He ran a hand gently along Legacy's neck, and after a few minutes the agitated horse began to calm down. Parker felt the stallion's legs carefully, then straightened and gave Allie an encouraging smile. "You'd think he'd never had a bath before," he joked.

Allie shook her head. "I shouldn't have pushed him at the jump," she replied. "He was spooked by the sunlight on the water and the current. I should have let him check it out before we tried to jump it."

Parker nodded. "It was really my fault," he said. "I wasn't even thinking about it. You had such great control of him that I just expected him to pop over it like it was nothing. I guess we overestimated his progress."

Allie led Foxy over to Parker and traded horses. "I'm sorry," she murmured to Legacy. The horse snorted and raised his head again, rolling his eyes. Allie ran her hand down his chest, murmuring a string of nonsense words in a calm tone, trying to help him settle back down. She glanced at Parker. "It's like he doesn't trust me anymore," she said. "Now what do we do?"

Parker pinched his lips together and eyed Legacy. "I'd say start from scratch," he said. "This is a setback, not the end of Legacy's jumping." He looked at Allie. "And it isn't the end of the bond you have with him, either. He just needs some time. I won't be around for a while to help you, but I'd start him in the arena again, get him used to the jumps, then expose him to water a little at a time until he doesn't think anything of it. You'll get there."

Allie shivered again, and Parker peeled off his jacket. "Wear this," he said. "It'll help a little."

Allie pulled off her own sodden coat and gratefully slipped into Parker's warm jacket.

"Are you ready to mount up?" Parker asked. "We still need to get back to Whisperwood."

Allie looked down at her waterlogged clothes and grimaced. "It's a good thing I brought a change of clothes for the party," she said, stepping to Legacy's side. As she tried to get her foot up to the stirrup, her jeans caught and pulled, and she gave Parker a pleading look. "Leg up?" she asked.

Laughing, Parker stepped beside her and cupped his hands so that she could step up and swing over Legacy's back. She shifted on the saddle and wrinkled her nose. "I'm glad I keep my tack well oiled," she said. "But even so, it's going to take some work to get this saddle dried out and reconditioned."

Parker swung back onto Foxy.

"I really blew it with that jump," Allie said regretfully.

Parker shook his head. "Legacy will get over it."

"How long is that going to take?" Allie asked. Even as she spoke she knew Parker had no way to answer the question.

"Look at Ozzie," Parker said, referring to his talented jumper. "When I got him, that horse would have been more likely to moo like a cow than take a jump."

"No way," Allie said, shaking her head in disbelief. "He'll jump anything."

"Now he will," Parker replied. "But he was completely burned out by too much time in competition. It seemed like it took forever to get his mind straight about jumping, but looking back, every day I spent working with him was worth it."

"I get it," Allie finally said. "Not that Legacy is ever going to be a competitive jumper, but I won't give up on him."

"That's good," Parker said. "There are a lot of excellent jumpers around that are by his sire and grandsire, so it would be a good selling point for his stud services to be able to show people that he can go over a fence as well as set some solid fractions on the flat."

Parker had a point. Legacy was good on the track. He just hadn't spent enough time there to make a name for himself. The Legacy foal Sterling was expecting would be their first chance to see if Legacy could pass some of the other talents of his ancestors on to his offspring.

Allie focused on Legacy's behavior as they rode back to Whisperwood. By the time they reached the farm, the horse was much calmer and more responsive to Allie, and she felt encouraged by the progress they'd made during the short time.

When Allie saw Christina's car parked by the house she was startled. "I guess we're running pretty late," she said.

Parker nodded. "If you want to go change, I'll take care of Legacy for you."

Allie shook her head. "I always take care of my horse before anything else," she said firmly. "You have your other horses to take care of after you're done with

Foxy, so if you don't want to miss the party, I suggest you get moving, Mr. Townsend."

Parker nodded agreeably. "Yes, ma'am," he said with a grin, then led Foxy away.

Before changing out of her soggy outfit, Allie gave Legacy a quick, warm bath, then groomed him until he was dry and shiny. Once she had him safely in one of the unused stalls, munching on a flake of hay, she got her party clothes from the car and went to the house. Christina was stacking cartoon-character paper plates on the dining room table.

"What happened to you?" Christina asked, eyeing Allie's wet clothes. "It's a little early in the year to be swimming."

"Remember when you jumped Legacy over that tree?" Allie asked. "I didn't do quite that well."

"He dumped you in the water?" Christina responded, her eyebrows raised in surprise.

"Worse," Allie said. "He dumped himself in the brook, and I bailed off."

"Hmmm," Christina said, frowning. "How did he handle it?"

"Not well," Allie said glumly. "Parker says we need to start the jumping lessons from scratch."

Christina tore open a bag of balloons, took a deep breath, and began inflating an orange balloon. As she tied the end she smiled at Allie. "You'll get it figured out. I know you will."

"Thanks," Allie said, although she didn't feel very confident about undoing the damage the failed jump had done to Legacy's confidence. "I need to take a quick shower and get changed, then I can help you with the decorations."

"Make it snappy," Christina said, glancing toward the kitchen as she lifted another balloon to her mouth. "Tor took the twins for a drive, and everyone should be here within an hour."

"I'll set a speed showering record," Allie promised, then hurried toward the bathroom and a quick hot shower. Soon she was back in the dining room, wearing a pair of black jeans and an emerald-green sweater, her hair washed and dried. The balloons were all inflated and scattered around the room like giant, brightly colored eggs, and Christina was moving some chairs around to make room for the guests.

"I'm ready to help," Allie announced.

"I've got things under control here, but Samantha could use you in the kitchen," Christina said, and Allie hurried in that direction. Soon she was frosting the cake Samantha had cooling on the counter, then used tubes filled with colored icing to decorate the top. Finally she stood back. "It isn't nearly as good as Luis could do, but I think I'm done."

Samantha glanced at the cake as she walked by with a tray piled with little sandwiches. "It's wonderful," she said, eyeing the two horses Allie had drawn freehand on the cake, leaping over the words *Happy Birthday Luke and Leah,* which she had arched into a jump. "I hope it tastes as good as it looks. But," she said, "there's one more thing to add." She held out a pair of candles shaped like the number 2, and Allie positioned them on the cake, then took it to the party table, where she made it the centerpiece.

When the rest of the visitors began to arrive, Allie joined the crowd gathering in the living room.

Beth and Ian came in the door, and Beth crossed the room to give Allie a hug. "How's my new granddaughter?" she asked.

"Great," Allie started to say, then remembered the disastrous ride. "Well, pretty good, anyway."

"Why's that?" Ian asked when he reached them.

Allie told them about the water jump, and Ian nodded. "Now that he's had a bad experience, it'll take a lot longer to get him to where he'll jump fearlessly," he said. "But with your skills, you'll get him past it in no time. I'm sure of it."

Everyone else seemed to have no doubt that she'd get Legacy past the failed jump. Allie wished she felt as sure of herself as the rest of the family did.

"Thanks, Ian. I mean, Grandpa," Allie said.

Ian grinned at her. "I do like the way that sounds."

Ashleigh and Mike came into the house, followed by Cindy and Ben, and Melanie.

"Kevin's running late," Melanie announced. "He had to go into town to get presents." She rolled her eyes. "And to think I've always been the one who can't get it together on time."

Christina laughed. "At least he remembered before he got here," she said.

Soon everyone was drinking punch, talking about the progress their horses were making, and planning upcoming races.

"This is going to be Royal Blue's year to be Whitebrook's star of the track," Ashleigh said.

Christina nodded. "I can hardly wait for my second

series of Triple Crown races," she said, then looked at Cindy. "How about Tall Oaks?" she asked.

Cindy shook her head. "Not this year," she said. "We thought about running Alpine Meadow, but I just don't want to put that kind of stress on her. By next year we'll have a few coming three-year-olds that we can consider for the Derby."

At the sound of footsteps on the porch, the conversation stopped and everyone looked at the door expectantly, waiting for the twins' entrance. But it was Kevin who scurried through the door, his arms loaded with bags.

"What did you do," Beth asked, "buy out the toy store?"

Kevin grinned at his mother. "I wish I were a kid again," he said. "They have so many great toys, I couldn't just pick one for each of them."

"Let's get them wrapped," Melanie said, taking one of the bags.

"Tor and the kids were coming up the drive behind me," Kevin said. "We don't have a lot of time."

"Use my bedroom," Samantha told him. "But you'd better hurry."

Kevin and Melanie left the room just as the door swung open again, and Leah flew into the room, her eyes bright. "Party!" she squealed. "Party!"

"Yay!" Luke exclaimed, coming in behind her. Ian scooped Luke up as Tor shut the door.

The twins' father gave the group a dazed look before his eyes settled on Samantha. "They're bundles of energy," Tor said. "I can barely keep up with them."

Samantha laughed as Leah dashed up to her, her arms up. "They do keep you going, don't they?" she confirmed, swinging Leah into the air, then giving her a kiss on the forehead.

Soon Kevin and Melanie came back to the room with the hastily wrapped presents, which they piled with the ones the others had brought. Samantha pointed out the food on the table. "Help yourselves," she said. "The birthday party has officially started."

Before long it was time to sing "Happy Birthday." Then Tor solemnly lit the candles, and everyone watched while the twins blew them out with Tor and Samantha's help.

"No!" Luke exclaimed as Samantha approached the cake with a knife.

"But we have to cut it to eat it," Samantha explained to him. "It's yummy chocolate cake."

Luke frowned thoughtfully, then nodded. "Cut," he said, pointing at the cake.

"Open," Leah added, gazing longingly at the stack of gifts on the dining room floor.

"I'll take care of the cake," Allie offered, taking over so that Samantha and Tor could help the twins with their gifts. They eagerly tore into their presents, but once the gifts were out of the boxes, they both began playing with the empty packages, using them as stalls, jumps, and trailers for some of the toy horses they'd been given.

Kevin watched, shaking his head in bewilderment. "I got them a whole stable setup complete with little plastic jumps and fences," he said, watching Luke cram a stuffed pony into a too-small box.

Ian laughed. "I remember when you and Christina were that age," he said. "You weren't any different."

Christina watched Leah try to feed a plastic horse a bit of frosting. "I can believe that," she said. For several minutes they watched the twins enjoy their toys, until finally Leah picked up her stuffed horse and crawled into her mother's lap. A minute or so later

Luke carried a book over to Kevin and held it up. "Read now," he said, and Kevin obliged, turning the pages and pointing at the different animals on each page.

"They'll sleep like logs this afternoon," Samantha predicted. She looked around at the group of adults. "Thanks so much for making this a great party for the kids."

"It was fun for us, too," Mike said from the sofa, where he sat with his arm draped over Ashleigh's shoulder.

When the phone rang, Tor went into the kitchen to take the call. He returned several minutes later, a strained look on his face. "That was Helen," he said. "She and Dad wanted to make sure the kids knew they were thinking of them today. She also said we need to check today's mail because the twins' birthday presents should be here."

"How are she and your dad doing?" Ian asked. Tor's father's health had started to fail while Tor and Samantha were working in Ireland several years earlier. When they returned to the United States to run Whisperwood, Mr. Nelson and Helen, his new wife, had moved to Arizona to retire.

Tor looked grim. "Dad isn't doing so well," he said. "Helen asked me not to let him know that she told me, but she suggested I take a trip to Flagstaff to see him." He shook his head. "I can't go," he said, looking at Luke on Kevin's lap.

Allie watched Samantha's expression while Tor shared his news. Sam's mouth tightened into a thin line, and she gazed steadily at her husband. Then she handed a drowsy Leah to Beth and went to Tor's side, putting her hand on his arm. "You can go," she said, looking into his face. "You have to. The kids and I will be fine."

"I can't go off and leave you to take care of everything," Tor protested. "There's so much going on with the farm right now, and the twins are a full-time job all by themselves."

"There's no argument," Samantha said firmly. "I'll manage just fine."

Allie thought of the newspaper article that would be coming out that week, the article Parker had insisted promote Whisperwood. Things could get pretty busy around the farm if Maureen's story attracted as much attention as Parker hoped it would, and Allie couldn't imagine how Samantha would handle it all.

She gnawed at her lower lip for a second, then stepped forward. "I have a week off for winter break," she said. "I can stay here and help."

Tor stared at her for a moment. "You can't do that," he said. "You have horses to work at Tall Oaks."

"I think it's a great idea," Cindy said.

"I can cover for you at Tall Oaks," Melanie told Allie.

"And of course we'll all be available to give Sammy a hand, whatever she needs," Beth said, nodding.

"See?" Samantha looked at Tor. "We have a great family to back us up, Tor. You need to go see your dad."

Luke's head was drooping, and Leah had her head pillowed on Beth's shoulder, her stuffed horse clutched to her chest.

"It looks like nap time to me," Ashleigh said, then turned to Tor. "And you need to call Helen, and the airline."

Tor's tense expression relaxed, and he lifted his hands in mock surrender. "I guess I'm outnumbered," he said.

"We'll put Luke and Leah to bed," Ian said, standing to lift Leah from Beth's lap. Kevin and Ian carried the sleepy toddlers to their room while Tor went back to the phone to make arrangements for his trip.

Allie began gathering up the strewn boxes and wrapping paper from the floor, and Cindy bent down to help her.

"This is really going to help Sammy and Tor out," she said. "Are you sure you don't mind giving up your vacation week?"

"I'm not giving it up," Allie said. "I'm glad I get a chance to give something back after everything Samantha and Tor have done to help me."

Samantha walked by, carrying a pile of paper plates to the kitchen. "You're a lifesaver, Allie," she said with a grateful smile.

Allie grinned up at her aunt. "I'll be spending time with my cousins," she told Samantha. "What better way to spend winter break than playing ponies with them?" She busied herself stuffing a bunch of wrapping paper into an empty bag. As she rose she saw Cindy looking at her.

"I'm proud of you," Cindy said.

Allie shook her head. "This is about family." She started to carry the bag toward the kitchen, then stopped and looked back at Cindy. "Being there when your family needs you is the most important thing of all."

7

TOR GOT A FLIGHT OUT OF THE KEENELAND AIRPORT THE following day, and Allie found herself immersed in life at Whisperwood. Between the active twins, helping Samantha with the riding lessons, keeping an eye on the expectant broodmares, and trying to work with Legacy, her days were full.

"You're such a help," Samantha told her one morning after Allie had taken over the beginning riding lessons while Samantha handled the flood of calls after the article about Parker and the Olympic team came out. "I don't know how I'd have managed without you here."

The last of the students had left the barn, and Samantha was helping Allie pick up the equipment in the indoor arena. Allie picked up another cavalletti pole and grinned at Samantha. "I'm having a great time," she said. "I'm glad I could be here to give you a hand."

"Oh, you've done more than just give me a hand," Samantha replied. "Luke and Leah adore their cousin Allie. You're fantastic with the kids."

"They're loads of fun," Allie said, stacking the last of the poles against the arena wall.

Kaitlin had finished cleaning the stalls and was in Samantha's office, watching over the twins and taking phone messages for Samantha. "I was really happy that Whisperwood got such great publicity," Samantha said. "But the timing was a little off, with Tor having to leave."

Allie finished dismantling the jumps from the lesson and nodded. "It'll be nice when he gets home," she said. "I'm glad his dad is doing okay. I know it must be tough for Tor, especially being so far away from his dad."

Samantha nodded. "It is," she said. "He's really close to his father, and it was hard to have Helen and him move so many miles away. I wish they could be around to spend time with their grandchildren. But," she added, "they're happy in Arizona, and that's what's important." She dusted her hands on the seat of her jeans. "Tor's dad was very supportive of us when we moved to Ireland. And if it hadn't been for those years we spent with the Hollis family, I don't think we'd be where we are now."

"A hugely successful training barn for eventing horses and riders," Allie noted.

Samantha smiled. "We're getting there," she said, then propped her hands on her hips and surveyed the arena. "It looks perfect," she said.

Allie gazed around the space and nodded thoughtfully. "Since Parker's going to be gone after next week, you're really going to have your hands full," she said.

Samantha sighed, sweeping a lock of her red hair back from her cheek. "I know. Everyone who read Maureen's article and has called wants lessons from me. They seem to think I personally taught Parker how to be a world-class eventer."

"Well," Allie said, "you did a lot to help him."

Samantha shook her head. "Parker had it inside himself to accomplish what he has. I just nudged him along a bit." She looked toward the row of stalls lining one wall of the arena. "I guess Whisperwood needs a full-time barn manager now. We've been doing really well, and this added attention to the farm is going to make us more popular than ever."

Kaitlin came out of the office. "Allie," she said, "Cindy's on the phone for you."

Allie hurried into the office and picked up the phone. "Hi, Mom," she said, propping her hip against the edge of the desk. She gazed at the sleeping twins and smiled. Kaitlin had been right. They were such busy little people, they kept her in constant motion when they were awake. The only time she really got a chance to enjoy watching them was when they were sleeping.

"Image dropped her foal," Cindy said breathlessly. "She had a beautiful little chestnut colt who looks exactly like Champion."

Allie moved around the desk and sank onto the chair. "Did everything go all right?" she asked. Since this was Image's first foal, everyone at Tall Oaks had been a little anxious, waiting to see how well she handled the birth.

"Perfect," Cindy replied. "She and Perfection are

doing great. He got right to his feet and started to nurse, and Image is going to be an excellent mother."

"I knew she would," Allie said proudly. "Was Melanie there?"

"She helped the vet," Cindy said. "She just left to go buy the baby a brand-new halter."

After she got off the phone with Cindy, Allie went back out to the arena to share the news with Samantha and Kaitlin.

"That's wonderful," Samantha said. "I hope our mares' foalings go as well."

"Congratulations," Kaitlin said. "I have to leave now, but I'll be back tomorrow."

"I'll take over babysitting," Samantha told her. "Thanks for helping out this morning, Kaitlin."

"No problem," Kaitlin said. "I'll see you guys later."

After the other girl had left, Samantha turned to Allie. "While we have a bit of a lull, do you want to run over to Tall Oaks to see the new foal?"

Allie gnawed at her lower lip. "I'll wait a little while," she said. "I'm sure Image is tired, and there'll be lots of visitors. If it's all right with you, what I'd really like to do is take Legacy out for a hack."

"Of course," Samantha said. "You haven't left the arena with him since the twins' party."

Allie nodded. "I've been a little worried that I'll do more things to set him back, and then we'll both be completely discouraged."

Samantha laughed. "Well, you won't know where you're at with him until you try, you know. You can't let one little bump in the road stop you."

Allie scrunched her face. "You sound so sensible," she told Samantha.

"Just take him for a leisurely hack, and maybe walk him near the stream, but don't try any jumps," Samantha advised. "Make it a calm ride. Then tomorrow you can try him over some brush jumps, and so on."

"Okay," Allie said. She really did want to ride on the trails, and she knew she was being foolish by avoiding taking Legacy out. If he did have a problem, not giving him a chance to overcome his fear wasn't going to help the situation.

She saddled the horse and soon was riding him along the same trail she and Parker had taken on the day of the birthday party. The weather was cool, but the sun was shining, and the budding leaves on the trees rustled softly overhead. Legacy sniffed the air, tossing his head and prancing a little, and Allie patted his neck. "I think I'm the one who's spooked, not you," she said, moving him into a smooth canter. The ride was pleasant, and Allie began to think she had overreacted to Legacy's tumble in the water. "Maybe it won't be a problem for you," she said, turning him onto a path that would take them near the stream.

She thought of the newborn foal at Tall Oaks and wondered how much longer it would be before Sterling and Miss Battleship had their babies. "Spring is such a nice time," she told Legacy. "Everything that's been asleep all winter wakes up. It all feels like new again."

She could hear the running water as they came out of the woods, and could see the bank of the stream winding through the meadow. Legacy pricked his ears and raised his head at the sound of the running water. He slowed, his strides becoming hesitant.

"You're all right," Allie told him, stroking his neck as they got even closer to the stream, but as soon as he saw the splashing, gurgling water sliding over the rocks, Legacy snorted and snapped his head up, then shied away.

Allie gripped his back with her knees, balancing

easily despite his sudden move, but disappointment settled heavily over her. The bad jump had been more traumatic for Legacy than she had wanted to believe.

"It's okay," she murmured, petting his neck soothingly as she circled him, not letting the horse bolt away from the water. She felt her heart sink as Legacy rolled his eyes, trying to scoot away from the sight and sound of the stream. "We're just going to ride past it, okay?"

It took several minutes, but finally Legacy walked close to the water, all the while dancing and tossing his head, snorting loudly as he tried to keep as much distance between the moving water and himself as he could.

When she finally got him to lower his head and relax a little, she felt as though she'd done all she could for the day.

"All right," Allie said, patting his shoulder as she turned him back toward the trail through the woods. "That was a good start, boy. We'll stick with fences and brush for a while before we go after the water again. We have all the time in the world." But deep inside she was afraid she'd never get Legacy over his fear of running water. And even though Parker had tried to take some responsibility for the disastrous jump, she knew Legacy's problem was all her fault.

When they returned to Whisperwood, Allie rode Legacy along the back of the barn so that she could see the broodmares. Sterling was in her turnout, her sides bulging. She was pressed up against the fence, looking toward the woods, her ears pricked, her head up and alert.

"You miss going out to the trails, don't you?" Allie said as she stopped Legacy near the turnout. Sterling stared past her, as if she knew where Allie and Legacy had been, and Allie felt bad for the mare.

"After your foal is weaned, maybe I can take you out again," she told Sterling.

As they rode past Sterling, Allie noticed that one of the boards looked as though it had pulled loose from the fence post.

"Probably from you leaning on it," she told Sterling. She stopped Legacy and hopped to the ground to check the loose rail. As she wiggled it, the long board came off in her hands. Sterling leaned further over the fence and nudged at Allie. Without the top rail in place, the fence was barely as high as the mare's legs.

"That's no good," Allie muttered, giving Sterling a gentle push back. Even in her current condition, Sterling could easily hop over the fence if she wanted to. Allie shoved the damaged rail back into place, making a mental note to come right back with a hammer and some nails to reinforce the fence.

"I guess I get to be Ms. Fix-it while I'm here," she told Legacy and Sterling. She led the stallion past the other broodmares, stopping to take a quick look at Miss Battleship. Tor and Samantha had bought the mare before they went to Ireland, and when they returned to Whisperwood, they had used her to start their breeding program. For the fifth time, the bay mare was in foal to Finn McCoul. Except for Irish Battleship, their first daughter, each of the foals had been sold, and all were doing well in competition. Irish Battleship had proven herself to be a world-class eventing horse, and Allie knew Samantha and Tor were excited about the prospect of another champion foal by their two favorite horses.

Miss Battleship was circling in her turnout, nipping at her sides. While Allie watched, she stopped, pawed at the ground, then grunted loudly.

"Oh my gosh, she's in labor!" Allie exclaimed. "I need to tell Sammy!" She hurried back to the barn with Legacy.

"Sammy!" she called, looking around the barn, but no one answered. "They must have gone up to the house for lunch," she told Legacy, and quickly stripped his tack and put him in his turnout.

Allie dashed for the house, but when she opened the front door, all she could hear was the sound of the twins wailing.

Samantha was sitting on the sofa, holding Luke and Leah. Tears streamed down both the children's faces, and Samantha looked up at Allie and rolled her eyes. "Heartbreak," she said simply.

"What happened?" Allie asked. She had never seen the toddlers so upset before.

"While I was fixing lunch, Luke flushed a little toy horse down the toilet. I guess Leah thought it was a good idea, so she did the same thing. Then they wanted their toys back. When I told them that wasn't going to happen, they started crying." She smiled wryly. "And they miss their father."

Allie gazed at the twins, feeling a sympathetic tug in her heart.

"Hey, Leah," she said.

The little girl looked up at her and sniffled. "Gone," she said sadly.

Allie nodded and sat down next to Samantha. "Yup," she said. "Gone, but at least they have each other for company. And you still have Luke."

Leah rubbed at her damp cheek and nodded. "Luke," she said, reaching over to pat her brother.

"And Teabiscuit's here," Allie said. "Do you want to go see him?"

"Biscuit!" Luke said, wiping the tears from his face. "Now!"

"Oh!" Allie said, remembering why she had rushed to the house. "You need to get out to Miss Battleship," she told Samantha. "I think she's in labor."

Samantha rose, depositing both the twins on Allie's lap. "I'll call the vet from the barn," she said, and rushed out of the house.

"Now, let's go see Teabiscuit," Allie told the twins, though what she really wanted to do was race after Samantha and see what she could do to help with Miss Battleship. *You're doing what you can to help,* she reminded herself, getting the twins' jackets from a hook near the door.

When they got to the barn, Samantha already had Miss Battleship in one of the oversize foaling stalls.

"Dr. Lanum is on her way," Samantha said, standing near the stall door, watching the mare. She glanced at Allie. "She's acting perfectly normal," she said. "I expect it will be a routine delivery." She reached over to stroke the mare's neck, which was starting to darken with sweat. "Miss Battleship has always been a great broodmare, haven't you, girl?"

The mare swiveled her ears, then twisted around to nip at her side again.

Leah tugged at Allie's hand. "Biscuit?" she asked.

Samantha looked at the twins and shook her head. "You'd never know that ten minutes ago they were completely distraught," she said, chuckling.

Allie nodded. "I guess a short attention span can be a blessing sometimes," she said. "After a little ride on Teabiscuit, they should be ready for a nap."

"If you want to have them lie down on the cot in the office, you can stay out here with me and we'll see what Dr. Lanum has to say about Miss Battleship. We'll be doing foal watch tonight."

Allie nodded agreeably. "That'll be great," she said.

She felt a tug on her hand and looked down to see both Luke and Leah gazing up at her.

"Now," Luke said.

Allie smiled down at the little boy. "Let's go put a saddle on Teabiscuit and do some riding."

She looked back at Miss Battleship, then forced herself to turn away, slowly walking along the aisle with the twins, until they reached Teabiscuit's stall. The pony tried to crane his neck to put his head over the stall door, but his little nose barely reached the top of the wall. Allie reached in and rubbed his muzzle, then opened the stall door.

Teabiscuit lowered his head as Luke and Leah walked into the stall, and he nuzzled Leah's outstretched hand affectionately. "What a nice little guy you are," Allie said, clipping a lead on the pony's halter. While Luke and Leah stood by, she quickly groomed Teabiscuit, and for several minutes she led the twins around the arena on the agreeable pony.

By the time Dr. Lanum got to the barn, Luke and Leah's heads were drooping. Allie quickly untacked their pony, then carried the twins to Samantha's office and settled them on the cot.

They were both sound asleep in minutes, and Allie hurried over to the foaling stall.

"Everything looks fine," the vet said, coming out of the stall as Allie walked up the aisle. "Miss Battleship is an old pro at this, aren't you, girl?"

The mare shifted, obviously uncomfortable.

"Any special instructions?" Samantha asked.

"Just keep an eye on her and give me a call when it looks like things are getting close," the vet directed her.

Allie watched her walk away, then turned to Samantha. "What do you need me to do now?" she asked.

"You can bring the other horses in," Samantha said. "We'll get chores taken care of early, and I'll call Chris to see if she wants to come over and do foal watch with us."

Allie was relieved. With Christina's training in veterinary medicine, it would be good to have her on hand, just in case of an emergency.

Allie left the barn to start bringing the rest of the horses in, while Samantha went to her office to call Christina.

When Allie went around the barn with Sterling's lead in hand, she stopped dead. The mare's turnout was empty. Allie saw the broken board lying on the ground outside the stall, and she stared for a minute, absorbing what she could see had happened. Sterling had gone over the fence. Allie looked around frantically, but there was no sign of the big gray mare. Sterling, who was due to drop her foal at any time, was gone!

8

ALLIE STARED AT THE WOODS, WHERE STERLING HAD BEEN gazing longingly earlier. Suddenly the peaceful copse of trees looked dark and threatening, dangerous for a lone mare who was about to have a foal. Allie had never seen any wild animals larger than birds and squirrels when she rode the trails, but she knew that Kentucky had its share of cougars, bears, and other wild creatures that might harm Sterling. The cool weather, which had seemed pleasant earlier in the day, felt chilly. Too cold for Sterling's foal, and the daylight wouldn't last much longer. They had to find Sterling, and there wasn't any time to waste.

The rest of the horses forgotten, Allie wheeled around and raced back to the barn. She saw Samantha coming out of her office as she dashed up the aisle. "She's gone!" she cried, skidding to a stop in front of Samantha.

"What?" Samantha caught her by the shoulders. "Who's gone?"

"Sterling," Allie gasped, fighting back tears. "It was all my fault. I knew the fence was broken, but when I saw Miss Battleship in labor, I forgot all about it. Sterling knocked the rail down and got out. She's gone, Sam! I know she took off into the woods."

"Calm down," Samantha said, releasing her grip on Allie's shoulders. "This is her first foal, and if she's in labor, her instinct would be to go someplace private and hidden."

"I'll look for her," Allie said. "I'll go saddle Legacy."

Samantha nodded, immediately turning back toward the office. "I'll call Whitebrook again and tell them we need help over here." Over her shoulder she added, "We'll get her back, Allie. Everything is going to be fine."

Allie wished she could believe Samantha, but at the moment she wasn't sure that anything was going to go right.

She raced out to Legacy's turnout, her hands trembling as she clipped his lead to his halter. "We have to find Sterling fast," she told him, throwing a pad on his back, then quickly setting his saddle in place. In a minute the stallion was ready to go. As she led him toward the door Christina walked into the barn.

"Going for a ride?" she asked, sounding surprised. "I thought we were doing foal watch on Miss Battleship."

"Sterling took off," Allie said tersely. "We need to get her back to the farm before she decides to have her foal on her own."

Christina's eyes widened. "I'll go with you," she said. "Give me a minute and I'll get Irish Battleship saddled."

Samantha came out of the office as Christina set off at a jog toward Irish Battleship's stall.

"I'll call Kaitlin and see if she can give me a hand here," Samantha told Allie. "She can keep an eye on the twins while I take care of the horses. Dad and Kevin are on their way over, and I've called the vet in case we need her." She thrust her cellular phone at Allie. "Take this. If you find her—" She stopped and shook her head. "*When* you find her, call."

As soon as Christina had Irish Battleship saddled, she and Allie rode out to Sterling's turnout. Allie leaned over Legacy's shoulder, looking at the ground. "It's hard to tell which tracks are hers," she said. "The ground is pretty torn up."

"She'd go someplace she knows," Christina said. "Which trails did you ride her on the most?"

Allie pointed at a path through the woods. "Kaitlin rode her a lot more than I did, and that's her favorite trail." She looked up at the sky. "It's going to get dark pretty soon."

"Then let's go," Christina said, urging Irish Battleship into a smooth trot. "Sterling wouldn't have done more than walk, so she can't have gotten far. We'll get her in time."

Christina's words did little to comfort Allie as they followed the trail into the woods. Allie searched the shadows under the trees, hoping to catch sight of the runaway mare, but as they got farther away from Whisperwood, she grew more and more concerned. "How far would she have gone?" she asked Christina.

"I don't know," Christina said, peering into the woods. "We'll just keep going. There's nothing else we can do."

The longer they rode, the more anxious Allie felt. "The sun is starting to go down," she fretted. "She can't be out here in the dark."

Christina nodded grimly. "Especially if she's in labor," she said.

Allie pointed at a side trail that meandered deeper into the woods. "Let's go that way. Kaitlin used to ride her along this trail. Irish Battleship and I rode with them a couple of times."

Christina looked at the wide trail ahead of them, then at the path Allie had indicated, and nodded, then guided Irish Battleship onto the narrow trail. They rode through the woods in tense silence, straining to hear any sounds Sterling might make, their eyes fixed on the underbrush and ground, searching for hoof-prints that might belong to the missing mare. But they didn't see anything helpful, and Legacy and Irish Bat-tleship continued on, not giving any sign that they sensed another horse nearby.

The coming twilight deepened the shadows, and Allie slowed Legacy, looking for any indication that a large animal had gone off the path and into the under-brush. "There's nothing," she moaned. "I don't see anything."

"There!" Christina exclaimed, pointing ahead of them on the path. "Do you see those bent branches?"

Allie heaved a sigh of relief and urged Legacy toward the place that Christina had pointed to. But when she looked at a tree just off the trail, her throat closed up. "It wasn't a horse," she told Christina. "Look at the marks on that tree."

"What did that?" Christina asked, staring at the torn bark several feet off the ground.

"It's an elk rub," Allie said. "My dad showed me a lot of those when we went camping. I don't think an elk would bother a horse, but if that's what we've been following, we're way off track."

Discouraged, they returned to the main trail and rode farther away from Whisperwood. Allie was afraid they would never find the mare in time, but she struggled not to let Christina know how worried she was.

Suddenly she spotted something on the ground, and sat up straight in the saddle. "Look," she said, pointing at the mark. "A shod horse went off the trail here, and the mark looks pretty fresh. It had to have been Sterling."

They turned onto the narrow, overgrown path, following the trail through the deepening woods.

In front of Allie and Legacy, Irish Battleship lurched, and Christina pulled the mare up and dismounted, bending over the big jumper's left front leg. "Oh, no!" she exclaimed. "I can't believe it." Christina straightened up, a grim look on her face.

"What's wrong?" Allie asked, gnawing at the inside of her mouth. Things seemed to be going from terrible to worse. If Irish Battleship had gone lame now, they'd have even more problems to deal with.

"Her shoe is loose," Christina said. "She must have caught it on a root." She checked Irish Battleship's hoof again and shrugged. "It's still in place, so I say we keep going. As long as we take it easy, she should be okay." She remounted, and they continued on the steadily narrowing trail.

Well off the path, Allie saw a large patch of gray nestled in the green underbrush, hidden by a clump of trees, and she rose in her stirrups, her breath locked in her chest as she stared at the shadowed place. When the patch moved, she nearly screamed with relief.

"There!" Allie exclaimed, urging Legacy off the barely visible trail and into the thick brush. As she came around a cluster of saplings, she saw Sterling. The mare was on her side, breathing hard. When

Legacy approached, she raised her head, grunted, then flopped back to the ground. Allie leaped from Legacy's back, her emotions a mixture of relief at finding the mare and terror that they hadn't gotten there soon enough.

"Sterling!" Christina gasped, vaulting from Irish Battleship's saddle. She tied the mare to a cluster of brush and hurried over to where Sterling lay helpless on the ground, Allie right on Christina's heels.

Allie moved to Sterling's head, cradling the mare's gray muzzle on her lap while Christina quickly checked the mare over, then felt her heart sink to her toes when Christina looked up at her in dismay. "She's too far into labor to get her back to Whisperwood," she said. "I'm not a vet, but I think she's going to have the foal anytime now." She paused. "If she can survive it."

At her words, Allie felt horror charge through her like an electric shock. "No!" she cried. "We can't just let her die!"

Christina nodded toward the cell phone Allie had clipped to her jeans. "Call the farm," she said. "We'll get the vet out here." She glanced around. "I know this area," she said. "I used to come through here from Whitebrook when I'd bring Sterling over to ride with

Samantha. Tell them we're near the old service road, the one with the red gate. Sammy'll know what I'm talking about."

Allie whipped the phone out and pressed the call button, then stared in dismay at the lighted display. "There's no phone service here," she said frantically. "I can't call out."

Christina tightened her lips. "You can ride back to the farm and get someone out here to help, but I don't think we have enough time. If we're going to have any chance to help Sterling and this baby, it's going to take both of us. Can you handle it?"

Allie stared at her. She'd do whatever she had to in order to help Sterling and the foal, but she didn't know the first thing about emergency deliveries. There'd been a veterinarian and several experienced adults around for every foaling she'd ever seen. She'd never so much as been in the stall when a mare gave birth. "I can't—" she started to say.

Christina silenced her with a sharp gesture. "You can," she said. "We have to. We're Sterling and her foal's only hope."

Allie swallowed a nervous lump. "Then tell me what to do," she said.

Time seemed to stop moving as Allie huddled over Sterling's head, stroking the mare, making soothing sounds, and trying to keep her from thrashing around while Christina examined her more closely. When the mare groaned in pain, Allie wanted to break down in tears. Instead, she continued to comfort Sterling, focusing on keeping her voice calm and relaxed, her hands light on Sterling's sweat-soaked coat.

Suddenly Sterling let out a low groan, and Christina gave a gasp. "It's almost over," she said. After what felt like an eternity to Allie, Christina exhaled heavily. "She's here," she said. "Sterling has a filly."

"Did you hear that?" Allie whispered into Sterling's ear. "You've got a little girl."

Sterling let her head rest heavily on Allie's lap, not even trying to get to her feet or look for her newborn foal. "Come on, girl," Allie urged her. "You need to get up and take care of your baby." She pushed at Sterling's head. "Get up," she said more firmly. But Sterling gazed up at her, and Allie could tell the mare was too drained to do anything.

"How's the baby?" she asked Christina, looking over Sterling's side.

But Christina didn't answer, and Allie was horrified

to see her friend working feverishly over the motionless filly.

"She's not breathing," Christina said, sounding as if she couldn't believe what she was saying.

"You have to do something," Allie said. "Isn't there something you can do?"

She watched Christina lean over the filly and pound her ribs with her fists, then bend down to put her mouth to the delicate muzzle. After Christina had repeated the action a few times, Allie realized she was trying to resuscitate the foal. She clenched and unclenched her fists, fighting for every breath she took, willing the filly to inhale, to move, to be all right.

It isn't going to happen, she thought in terror. *Sterling has lost her foal.* Allie fought to stop herself from bursting into tears.

"Yes!" Christina exclaimed.

Allie looked up to see the filly's long, fragile legs give a kick, and Christina straightened, her eyes bright with relief. "She's breathing now," she said.

Allie peeled off her jacket and held it out. "Use it to rub her down," she told Christina. "We need to get her circulation pumping."

She continued to comfort Sterling while Christina

massaged the filly, rubbing her thoroughly in brisk, circular motions.

"Now we have to get Sterling up," she said.

"How?" Allie asked. "She doesn't even want to try."

"Help me here," Christina said, and Allie let Sterling's head rest against the ground while she moved to Christina's side. They carefully lifted the foal, whose gangly legs kicked weakly, and put the baby near her dam's head.

Sterling lifted her head, running her tongue over the filly's coat. She tried to get to her feet, but she was too exhausted to do more than kick feebly.

"You have to go for help," Christina told Allie urgently. "Don't waste any time."

Allie hesitated. If something happened to Sterling and the foal after she left, she'd never forgive herself.

"Now!" Christina ordered her. "Go!"

Allie scrambled to her feet and hurried back to where Legacy and Irish Battleship were tied, feeling as though she was deserting Christina. She looked back at Sterling and saw Christina huddled over the mare and foal, then turned away. She didn't have a choice. She had to ride for help.

Allie looked longingly at Irish Battleship for a moment, knowing that the bay, experienced in cross-country, would be the best horse to take. But with a loose shoe, she might end up lame before they even got close to Whisperwood, and then she'd never get to the farm in time to get the help Sterling and the baby desperately needed.

She turned to Legacy. "It's up to you," she said, freeing his reins from the bushes. "We have to save Sterling and your foal." She flung herself onto his back and turned him, pressing her heels into his sides. "Let's go," she said, gathering the reins and leaning over his withers.

Legacy responded to the familiar cues, cantering along the narrow path with Allie crouched over his back. When they reached the main trail, Allie pushed him into a gallop. Riding so fast was risky in the growing darkness, but Legacy was sure-footed, running steadily along the path.

As they neared another branch on the trail, she debated taking the longer route. Then her mind flashed back to the filly lying limply in Christina's arms and Sterling with her head resting on the ground. They didn't have any time to waste.

"This way," she cried, turning Legacy onto the

shortcut she and Parker had taken the day of the disastrous ride. Legacy covered the ground with long, powerful strides, and as they approached a low fence, Allie gathered the reins and positioned herself, her teeth gritted as she prepared for a clumsy jump or, worse, a refusal. But Legacy sailed over the fence without missing a stride, and Allie felt her confidence soar.

"We're going to be fine," she told Legacy, guiding him over another jump. The stallion seemed to pick up on Allie's urgency, and his training as a racehorse kicked in. He stretched low to the ground, charging across the fields, showing no hesitation as they cleared obstacle after obstacle.

"Parker should see you now!" Allie exclaimed as Legacy cleared a brush jump and kept running. If only this weren't such an awful situation, if only they weren't racing to save Sterling and her foal, she knew this would be the most exhilarating ride of her life.

Then she saw the snaking curve of the stream bank, and she tightened her grip on the reins, her heart clenching with fear. What if Legacy panicked again? What if he refused to jump the water? What if he hurt himself this time? She should have taken the easier trail back to Whisperwood. It would have taken longer, but it would have been a sure thing. "What was I thinking?" she moaned.

Legacy continued at breakneck speed, but as they got closer to the water, Allie knew that if he refused at the rate he was going, they'd both get hurt, and if he slowed down, they'd never make the jump.

Legacy seemed to pick up on the tension she was telegraphing down the reins, and he raised his head a little, his neck tensing. She felt his gait falter. "It's me," she mumbled, trying to calm her mind. "It isn't you, boy, it's me. You'll do fine."

For Sterling, she told herself. *For Sterling and her filly, I have to calm down.* She envisioned Legacy sailing easily over the water without a flaw, and tried to send that image to the stallion.

For a split second she thought Legacy was going to wheel away from the stream, but then, as she continued to feed herself the image of a perfect jump, he picked up his strides again. As they neared the water Allie moved into position, forcing the thoughts of a successful jump into her mind.

"Let's go!" she cried, feeling the huge boost of energy as Legacy bounded into the air. But in the dark it had been hard to judge the distance, and even as they went soaring over the water, Allie could tell they had taken off too soon. They were going to land short of the far bank.

As Legacy's forelegs touched down on the bank, his hind legs hit the water. Allie knew they were going to crash. She tried not to think about the fall, keeping her weight forward over Legacy's shoulders, giving the horse his head. It was up to Legacy to save them now. She had to trust her horse. There was nothing else she could do.

9

Legacy stumbled, jerking the reins from her hands, and Allie's heart stuttered as she realized they were going down. A horrible vision flashed through her mind, and she cried out at the nightmarish image that filled her head.

Although she had never seen the tragic race, now, as clearly as if she'd been there, she saw her father, his horse slamming into the rail, then flipping over, breaking both legs and crushing Craig Avery beneath his weight. If he'd been able to get clear of the horse, he might have survived the wreck.

Allie gasped and started to kick her feet out of the

stirrups, determined to fall free of Legacy when he went down. Beneath her, she felt the stallion scrambling to keep his footing. The horse was doing everything he could to keep from failing her, fighting valiantly to stay up. The realization stilled Allie. She sat motionless so that she wouldn't interfere with Legacy, letting her trust in her horse take over.

As if a terrible weight had been lifted from her, she felt a sudden calmness, a sense of being one with her horse. With one more lunge, Legacy moved forward, regaining his balance. With an incredible burst of power, the stallion charged up the bank, away from the water, and without hesitating continued to run, galloping with all the speed he had along the fence that skirted Whisperwood.

"We're going to make it!" Allie cried, overjoyed with Legacy's success. She quickly collected the reins and adjusted her seat, leaning over his shoulders again, urging him forward. Legacy hugged the fence line as he raced swiftly toward home, and Allie shifted her hands up on his neck, rising in the stirrups. Even in the dark, she knew the horse was going to get them back to Whisperwood safely.

No one would ever see Legacy move like this on a

racetrack, but she knew her horse was running the greatest race of his life. And it didn't matter whether someone was timing his fractions or not. Legacy was as much a champion as any of Wonder's other foals who had earned fame on the racetrack.

When she saw the roofline of Whisperwood's barn come into view, she turned Legacy, slowing him as they neared the paddocks. As they continued along the wide tractor lane between the pastures, she saw people coming out of the barn, backlit by the light spilling from the doorway.

She pulled Legacy to a stop as Mike reached up and caught the horse's headstall. Legacy pranced, tossing his head and snorting, his breathing heavy and his muscles quivering with exhaustion.

"Where's Chris?" Mike demanded as Allie jumped from Legacy's back. "I've got the trailer ready to go."

In a rush of words, Allie delivered Christina's directions. Mike left her holding Legacy and dashed back to the barn, shouting for Kevin and Ian.

Allie led Legacy inside in time to see Mike, Kevin, and Dr. Lanum running out the door. The truck engine roared to life, and the three men sped away from the farm, the empty trailer rattling behind them.

Allie sagged against Legacy's shoulder. "We made it, boy," she whispered, pressing her head to his sweat-soaked neck. "You did it. You ran the longest, toughest race of your life, and you came through."

Ian hurried over to them, running his hand expertly down Legacy's chest and legs. "We need to walk him out," he said, stripping the stallion's saddle from his back. "Start circling the arena, and I'll grab a cooling sheet for him." He paused to pull his jacket off and throw it over Allie's shoulders, then strode toward the tack room.

After the exertion of the long ride, Allie felt a chill settle into her shoulders. She tugged the heavy barn coat closed, then began leading Legacy around the outside wall of the arena. "You did your best, boy," she murmured, patting his damp neck. "I'm so proud of you. All I needed to do was trust you a little."

Legacy grunted softly. Allie knew they'd done what they could, but she wondered if they'd made it in time to get Sterling and the foal the help they needed. All she could do was wait until Mike and the vet returned, and in the meantime take care of Legacy.

Ian returned with the cooling sheet, which he draped over the exhausted horse's back. "Miss Battleship had her foal," he announced. "A colt, handsome and healthy as can be."

"I'm glad," Allie said, smiling faintly, wishing she could be more excited about the new foal, but she was still overwhelmed with worry about Sterling and the other foal, the one who was lying in the woods, without soft bedding and the warmth of the barn.

Ian hugged her shoulder, keeping pace with her as she continued to walk Legacy out. "Christina will take good care of Sterling and the foal, Allie," he said.

Allie felt tears well up, and she swallowed around the lump in her throat. "I know," she mumbled. "Christina already saved the baby once, but what if . . . what if . . ." She couldn't bring herself to say it aloud, afraid that she might jinx whatever chance the tiny horse had.

"Everything will work out," Ian said reassuringly. He took Legacy's lead from her. "You go sit down for a while," he told her. "This has been a pretty stressful evening for you. I'll keep walking Legacy. We don't want him to stiffen up."

"But—" Allie started to protest. She always took care of her own horse.

Ian shook his finger at her. "That's Grandpa's orders," he said kindly but firmly.

Allie crossed the arena, still too wound up to sit still, and peered into the foaling stall to see Miss Battleship's baby.

The mare was standing close to the front of the stall, her head turned to her far side, and Allie had to look under her to see a set of long, sturdy legs, the legs of a future jumper. It was too shadowy in the stall to see much more, especially with the mare blocking her view.

"He's nursing," Samantha said as she came up beside Allie. "I'm sure when he's done, Miss Battleship will let you see him. She seems pretty proud of her new son."

At the sound of Samantha's voice, the big mare looked around, moving enough so that when Allie stepped to the side of the stall, she caught a glimpse of a stubby, frizzy light brown tail flapping energetically as the foal nursed.

She thought of Sterling's tiny chestnut filly, limp and helpless in the woods, and the tears she'd held back for the last few hours began to flow. The tension that had kept her going hit her all at once, and her legs started to tremble. She leaned against the stall, trying to keep her composure, but she was failing fast.

"Here," Samantha said gently, wrapping her arm around Allie. She led her to the office and pointed her at the chair behind the desk. "Sit here. It'll be all right, Allie. Mike and Dr. Lanum will be here soon with Sterling and the filly."

She left Allie alone in the office, and Allie rocked back and forth in the chair, hoping Samantha was right and that everything was going to be fine.

It felt like an eternity before she heard the truck pull up to the barn. As soon as the sound of the truck met her ears, she jumped from the chair and hurried out of the office. Mike was pulling the truck and trailer into the arena through the big double doors. He parked as close to the stalls as he could, and Allie waited anxiously as Ian swung the trailer gate open.

Allie was relieved to see Sterling standing in the trailer. Somehow they'd gotten her on her feet. The mare's head hung low, her eyes dull and listless, but she was up, and that was a good sign. Dr. Lanum was holding her head, and Christina was on the trailer floor, the filly on her lap. She looked up at Allie and smiled weakly. "We made it," she said. "Kevin stayed with Irish Battleship. Dad's got to go back and pick them up."

Ian stepped inside the trailer and took Sterling's lead, guiding the mare carefully onto the arena floor. To Allie's relief, Sterling twisted her head back, looking into the trailer at her foal, and nickered gently. She might have been weak and tired, but she still wanted to be near her baby.

Samantha took Sterling's head, pressing her face against the mare's long nose. "Don't you ever do anything like this again," she said. Sterling released a tired sigh.

"Let's get her in a stall so I can do a complete exam," Dr. Lanum said. She and Samantha led Sterling away while Ian lifted the tiny foal from Christina's arms and carried it out of the trailer.

"She's so little," Allie murmured, reaching out to touch the wide blaze running down the filly's dainty nose. The filly's huge, dark eyes were open, and she looked into Allie's face as though searching for something. Allie felt an instant tug on her heart. She reached up to smooth the puff of forelock between the filly's ears and trace the tufted strip of mane along her crest. The filly's legs dangled limply as Ian held her, and Allie could see the four stockings that covered her fetlocks.

She bit down a sob. The filly looked so weak, so fragile. Allie thought of Miss Battleship's sturdy, strong colt, his tail flapping happily as he ate, and she ran a hand down the little filly's fine, furry coat. "You're home and safe now, baby."

Ian nodded. "Once she gets a chance to move around, she'll get stronger by the minute. She's had a tough start, but I've known other horses who've pulled through and done well in spite of it all."

Christina gave Allie a tired smile as she climbed out of the trailer. "You did it, Allie. You and Legacy got help to us in time."

"*We* did it, you mean," Allie said. "If it hadn't been for you saving the baby in the first place, there wouldn't have been any reason for us to ride for help."

Christina wrapped her arms around Allie, and for a hopeful moment Allie felt as though everything really was okay. Sterling and the filly were home, and Dr. Lanum had things under control.

"You can bring her in to her mother now," Dr. Lanum called from the stall, where she was giving Sterling an injection. "Let's see if we can get her to nurse. She needs that colostrum if she's going to pull through."

Allie followed Ian to the stall, not wanting to take her eyes off the filly. Christina went with them, and while Dr. Lanum and Samantha reunited the mare and foal, Allie and Christina watched from outside the stall.

Ian gently lowered the filly to the floor, but as soon as her hooves touched the ground, her legs collapsed, and she crumpled in an untidy heap. Sterling lowered her nose and gave the filly's coat a stroke with her tongue.

"She's too weak to stand up," Christina said, sounding worried. "She's been through so much already. I know we're not supposed to intervene, but isn't there more we can do?"

Dr. Lanum looked up and shook her head. "Sometimes we have to let nature take its course. You know that, Chris. It's hard to do, but if she's too weak to survive, sometimes all we can do is buy a little more time. Sometimes in the end . . ." She didn't finish the sentence. She didn't need to.

Allie stared at the filly, knowing that no matter what the vet said, she'd do whatever she had to in order to help her survive. This was Legacy's daughter, and she deserved every chance in the world.

At the sound of the truck returning, Christina stepped away from the stall. "Kevin and Mike have Irish Battleship," she said. "I need to go take care of her."

Allie stayed by Sterling's stall while Christina met Kevin near the back of the trailer. Kevin led Irish Battleship into the arena as Mike climbed from the truck. He bent over to look at the mare's hoof.

"We'll get the farrier out here tomorrow," Mike said. "She didn't do any damage except to a little bit of hoof that got torn when the nail pulled loose. She'll be fine." He straightened and gazed at Christina and Allie. "You two are heroes," he said. "Both of you."

"Christina saved the filly, and Legacy's the one who ran his heart out to get help," Allie said. "If I'd gotten that fence board fixed, Sterling never would have gotten out in the first place. This is all my fault."

Mike shook his head. "I disagree," he told her. "You and Christina saved Sterling and her filly. You did a great job."

Christina reached for Irish Battleship's lead, but Kevin waved her away. "I'll take care of her for you," he said. "You've had quite a day already."

Christina gave him a grateful look. "I'll take you up

on that," she said. "I want to go take a hot shower." She walked away, her shoulders slumped and her head down.

Allie watched her go, then returned to the filly's stall. Dr. Lanum was leaving the stall, and she paused by the door to offer Allie a friendly smile. "We just need to give her time," she said, then turned to Samantha. "I'll leave you a list of instructions. Call me if anything changes." The two women headed for Samantha's office, leaving Allie alone at Sterling's stall.

She glanced around, seeing that everyone was busy, at least for now, and she let herself into the stall, settling on the floor next to the filly.

"You need to stand up," she said, stroking the foal's jaw gently. "Can't you at least try?"

The filly gazed up at her, her liquid eyes showing a keen intelligence, and Allie felt that funny tug at her heart again, as though the filly was communicating with her. But the tiny animal lay quietly, not attempting to move, and Allie felt the fear of uncertainty.

"I'm not going to let you lie here and give up," she told the filly. "Not now." She watched Sterling run her tongue over the filly's fuzzy coat again, and she reached up to stroke the mare's gray muzzle. "We're not going to give up on your baby, are we, Sterling?" She looked down at the filly again, stroking the white blaze that covered her delicately tapered nose. "And that means you'd better not give up on yourself."

10

Samantha and Dr. Lanum returned to the stall, and Allie looked up at them, her hands resting on the filly's sides, feeling each breath as her sides rose and fell. Their serious expressions filled her with fear for the foal.

The vet came into the stall and ran her hands over the filly, moving her legs, looking into her dark eyes. The filly didn't respond, but lay in a limp bundle as the vet examined her. Dr. Lanum's brow wrinkled into a concerned frown when she saw how listless the foal was.

"She's not looking too good," she told Samantha as

she exited the stall. "How much effort do you want to put into saving her?"

Allie looked up anxiously, watching Samantha's expression closely.

Samantha gazed down at the sickly foal, then smiled at Allie. "We need to give her every chance we can," she said.

Dr. Lanum looked into the stall, nodding slowly. "The odds aren't very good for her," she said. "Even if she survives, she might always be a weak, sickly horse." She looked at Samantha. "And you know as well as I do that it costs more to keep a poor horse healthy than it does to take care of a useful one. If you need me to . . ." Her voice trailed off.

Allie was horrified to hear Dr. Lanum put a dollar value on Sterling's filly, but she knew that the vet was only being practical. The problem wasn't that the vet was coldhearted. It was that the filly had already stolen Allie's heart, and she couldn't put a price on saving her. Only the filly wasn't Allie's to save.

Samantha gazed at Allie for a moment, then patted the vet's arm. "We'll let you know," she said.

As they walked away Allie stroked the foal's slender neck. "I'll do whatever I can for you, but you have to fight, too," she said urgently. The filly's dark eyes met hers, and for a moment the girl and foal gazed at each other. Then the filly closed her eyes and seemed to shrink a little. Allie bowed her head and tears began to flow, running down her cheeks and dripping onto the filly's soft coat.

"Please," she whispered. "Please." She ran her hands down the filly's neck and sides, reaching out to move the limp legs, her tears falling freely. "You have to want to do this. Don't you want to grow up big and strong like your sire and your dam?" The filly released a sigh, and for a horrible moment Allie thought she had taken her last breath. Then the foal gave a weak kick with her back legs, and Allie felt a fresh surge of hope.

"Maybe you should go up to the house and rest for a while."

Allie raised her head to see Samantha looking into the stall. She couldn't leave now. What if something happened to the filly after she left? "Not yet," she told Samantha.

Samantha's smile was tired. "There's nothing we can do," she told Allie. "Like Dr. Lanum said, we need to let nature take its course. I'd feel awful if you got too attached to her and she died anyway, Allie."

Allie gazed up at Samantha and gave her a sad smile. "It's too late," she said. "I'm already too attached, and I can't undo it."

Samantha stared at her for a minute, then walked away, leaving Allie alone with Sterling and the foal.

After she left, Allie continued to stroke the foal's slender neck. "We're not giving up," she said urgently. "I didn't give up on Legacy, and he came through for me. He risked his life to save you. If you've got any of his spirit and determination in you, you'll keep trying."

Sterling nuzzled the filly again, and Allie leaned down to touch a kiss on the filly's forehead. "Can't you try to stand up?" she begged. "If you'd just try, I know you could do it."

But the filly didn't move, and Allie felt dread tightening her chest. She couldn't bear the thought of losing the filly. Losing her parents had been so heart-wrenching that she knew she couldn't stand feeling that kind of pain again, and the filly had already worked her way so deeply into Allie's heart that she knew how much she'd suffer if the filly died.

"Well," another voice said, "this looks awfully familiar." The stall door opened, and Ashleigh slipped inside.

Allie looked up at the woman, waiting for her to repeat what the vet and Samantha had told her. But Ashleigh had a look of determination on her face, and Allie felt her heart lighten.

Ashleigh crouched down and petted the filly. "She looks just like Wonder did the day she was born. Weak and helpless and more dead than alive." But Ashleigh's tone didn't sound gloomy and somber, and her words didn't send Allie's mood spiraling down the way the vet's grim statement had.

Allie knew that when Ashleigh was twelve, living at Townsend Acres, no one had given Wonder much of a chance to survive after a difficult birth. But Ashleigh had stuck by the filly and saved her life, and in spite of the bad start, Wonder had grown up to be an incredible racehorse and broodmare.

"Let's help her up," Ashleigh said. "We'll see if we can get her to nurse." She smiled at Allie and winked. "I've done this before," she said. "And even though the adults told me it was a waste of time, Wonder and I proved them wrong."

Allie got to her feet, and with Ashleigh's help, they lifted the filly, supporting her while her tiny hooves barely touched the ground. Allie held her breath as they steadied the foal, letting her get used to the feeling of being upright. Her head hung down as though it weighed too much for her long, slender neck, and Allie reached under her chin, raising her head a little. "She's too weak," she said, giving Ashleigh a fear-filled look.

Ashleigh shook her head. "We're not giving up," she said. As they held the foal, she gave a weak kick of her legs, but when they tried to let her hold her own weight, her legs began to buckle. Ashleigh quickly held her up again, nodding. "The more she moves, the better things will get," she told Allie. "Now let's get her over to Sterling so she can try to nurse."

Carefully they maneuvered the filly to Sterling's side, and Ashleigh guided the tiny nose to her dam's milk-filled udder. Finally, after getting a taste of the milk, the filly began to nurse. Ashleigh kept her hand under her jaw, holding her head up while she ate.

"Yes," Allie said breathlessly. "Keep drinking,

baby. It'll make you strong." As the filly nursed, Ashleigh carefully moved her hand away from the filly's jaw, and Allie waited for the little head to drop again. But the filly kept eating, and Allie looked up at Ashleigh, feeling her heart lighten. "She's doing okay."

Ashleigh nodded. "Maybe we can pull this off," she said. "Only time will tell for sure." She smiled softly at the foal. "But we'll do whatever we have to, won't we?"

It seemed to Allie that it was too soon when the filly stopped eating and let her head loll, her eyes closing. The effort of just a few minutes of nursing had exhausted her.

"That's good for now," Ashleigh said, helping Allie settle the filly back on the bedding. "She's got a little colostrum in her, and pretty soon she'll be ready for more. I'm going to go talk to Samantha for a minute."

"I'll stay here," Allie said, sitting down again, resting her back against the stall wall.

"I figured as much," Ashleigh replied with a warm smile.

After Ashleigh left the stall, Allie began petting the filly's flank, softly humming a lullaby she remembered her mother singing to her when she was little. The filly's ears, too large for her head, flicked at the sound, and Allie knew that even though she was sound asleep, she was listening to the song.

Ashleigh returned several minutes later, a bottle in her hand. "I talked to Samantha," she said. "We don't want to fill Sterling's foal up with milk replacement, but you can feed her a little of this to help her get strong enough to stand up and nurse." She handed the bottle to Allie. "And when you need a break, let me know. I'll fill in for you."

Allie nodded, smiling up at Ashleigh and feeling more hopeful than she had for hours. "Thanks, Ashleigh," she said. "I'll be fine for now. I don't want to leave her."

Ashleigh left them alone, and when the foal began to stir again, Allie held the tiny filly's head on her lap and pressed the nipple to her lips, urging her to drink. "It's going to help you," she said. "Don't you want to grow up to be a big, strong racehorse?" As if she understood, the foal took a few swallows of the milk, then pulled away.

"Are you ready to try nursing again?" Allie asked, setting the bottle aside. "Your mother's milk will be better for you anyway." She put her arms under the foal's stomach and tried to get her to her feet again, but the filly was still too weak to stand.

Then the tiny creature blinked her eyes, nudging her nose toward the discarded bottle of milk. Allie grabbed the bottle and pressed it to the filly's mouth. "Drink," she said, feeling a tremor of hope as the filly licked the nipple. Allie squeezed the bottle, and a few drops of milk dripped into the filly's mouth. When she swallowed, Allie nearly screamed with excitement.

"Again," she said, tilting the bottle. The filly took another taste of milk, then struggled to lift her head. "That's it," Allie cried, helping her raise her head so that she could nurse.

"What's going on in here?"

At the sound of Ashleigh's voice, Allie looked up to see her face peering over the stall door. Ashleigh gazed at the foal for a moment, then slipped into the stall and dropped to her knees by the filly's side. "She's eating pretty well," she said, helping Allie hold the filly's frail neck up. "Keep her going, Allie. I'll help you."

After a few minutes, the filly grew tired again, and Allie's hope faded. "She didn't drink very much," she said, discouraged.

But Ashleigh smiled at her. "She drank enough for now," she replied, stroking the fuzzy brown flank. "Let her rest for a bit, then we'll get a fresh bottle and try it again."

Ashleigh settled onto the stall floor beside Allie. "I've been through this a time or two," she said. "Sometimes you succeed, and sometimes you get your heart broken. With Wonder, I succeeded, and this little girl has a lot of Wonder in her, so maybe she'll have the grit to pull through."

"Was it just like this with Wonder?" Allie asked, even though she was pretty sure she knew. She'd heard the story dozens of times from Cindy, who had ridden Wonder to a win in the Kentucky Derby. She eyed the foal again, trying to imagine the sickly baby all grown up and thundering along the racetrack, beating the country's best racehorses to the finish line. It didn't seem possible, but Ashleigh had done it with Wonder.

"Wonder," Ashleigh said fondly, a faraway look in her eyes. "She had a tough birth, and the vet didn't give her much of a chance. But everyone underestimated Wonder, and she proved them all wrong." Her expression darkened a little. "I think I expected a little too much from her, though," she added.

"Why was that?" Allie asked, running her hand down the filly's delicate nose, admiring the fringe of dark lashes that shaded her eyes. "She won the Derby and had lots of great foals. Didn't she do even better than you'd hoped?"

"Legacy was supposed to be Wonder's last foal," Ashleigh said, massaging the filly's tiny legs as she spoke, working them to encourage the circulation. "But she looked so healthy that after a year's rest, I decided to breed her one more time. If I hadn't done that, she would have lived several more years."

"But if you hadn't bred her, Star wouldn't be here now," Allie said.

Ashleigh nodded. "I didn't think about Star after I lost Wonder," she said. "I was so distraught, I couldn't think clearly for a long time."

"You?" Allie stared at her in amazement.

Ashleigh nodded, wrinkling her nose. "I blamed myself for Wonder's death, but every time I saw Star, I'd think that I'd wasted Wonder's life for a foal that wasn't going to make it." She shook her head. "I forgot my own experience with his dam, taking a foal no one thought would ever be worth anything and helping her become the best Thoroughbred I've ever known. I quit going out to the barn just to avoid seeing him because it broke my heart every time I was around him." She released a sad sigh. "I did a lot of things wrong."

"I can't believe that," Allie said. "You know more about horses than anyone."

Ashleigh chuckled. "I'm human, Allie. I make mistakes, and I don't always use the best judgment. Adults aren't any smarter than kids," she said. "We're just supposed to be a little wiser from years of living." She shifted a little and began gently pumping the filly's hind legs. "When I was young, my parents had a breeding farm, Edgardale. I thought I was living the perfect life there until a virus wiped out most of the stock and we lost the farm."

"That must have been horrible," Allie said.

Ashleigh nodded. "It was. We moved to Townsend Acres, which wasn't the nicest place in the world for me, but when Wonder was born, I knew everything was going to work out fine."

"So you'd lost horses you cared about before," Allie commented.

Ashleigh kept her eyes on the filly, smoothing the soft fur on her belly. "I had," she said. "But there was nothing I could do to prevent the virus, so when I was able to save Wonder, I felt like I had done something good. Breeding Wonder that last time was my choice, and I felt like I took her life when the foaling went wrong."

"But you didn't know anything would happen," Allie protested.

"I know," Ashleigh said. "And I made some horrible decisions about Star. I'm glad Christina was as determined as she was." She looked up and smiled fondly. "As stubborn as I was," she amended.

The filly opened her eyes again, and as Ashleigh released her leg, she gave a little kick.

"Did you see that?" Allie exclaimed. Before she had finished speaking, the filly gave another kick, then struggled to move her front legs.

"Give her some room," Ashleigh said, scooting back. "Let's see if she can get to her feet."

Allie slid away from the filly but stayed close by. As the foal scrabbled with her long legs on the stall floor, Allie and Ashleigh positioned themselves at her sides, ready to help support her if she needed it.

After a minute of trying, the filly fell back, exhausted again, but Ashleigh's broad smile kept Allie from being disappointed.

"Give her a little more milk," she said, and Allie offered the bottle to the foal once again.

The filly took the nipple and drank, this time with a little more energy than before.

"We're not out of the woods yet," Ashleigh cautioned Allie, "but things are looking better."

After a few more pulls on the bottle, the filly lay back, then began flexing her legs again, pressing her tiny hooves to the floor as she tried to get her front legs under her.

Allie held her breath, wanting to help the filly to her feet but knowing that the exercise was necessary for her to build the strength to stand on her own. Suddenly the foal was up, balancing unsteadily, a startled look on her face.

"I think she's surprised herself," Ashleigh said, getting to her feet. "I'm going to get Samantha. She has to see this."

Allie stayed by the filly's side, doing what she could to help her keep her balance. After a short time the filly collapsed in an untidy heap, but this time she kept her head up.

"You liked standing, didn't you?" Allie crooned, stroking her heaving side. "Pretty soon you'll be prancing around here like you own the place."

As if she liked the idea, the filly struggled to her feet again, then tottered to her dam's side and began to nurse on her own.

When Ashleigh returned with Samantha, Allie grinned up at them. "Isn't she wonderful?" she asked.

Samantha watched the filly nurse for a minute, then turned to Ashleigh. "She is wonderful, isn't she?"

Ashleigh nodded silently, unable to tear her gaze away from the foal. "She looks exactly like her granddam," she said softly. "She could be a little Wonder."

"We could name her that," Samantha said, looking at Ashleigh. "What do you think of A Little Wonder?"

If they were picking a name for the filly, Allie knew, they were as sure as she was that Legacy and Sterling's foal was going to be all right. Her heart soared, and she looked up at the two women. "Or maybe Legacy's Wonder?" she asked.

Ashleigh brushed at a tear that had started to slip down her cheek. "Allie's Wonder," she said. "I'd like it if you'd call her that."

As if she knew they were talking about her, the filly

turned away from her dam and looked at the three people, her ears pricked, her big eyes bright and alert. She let out a little nicker.

Samantha stared at the filly for a long moment, and Allie waited anxiously for her to say something. Then she smiled and nodded. "Allie's Wonder it is."

As if she knew the business of picking her name was finished, Allie's Wonder turned her back to the humans, pressing her nose against her dam's gray side. As Samantha, Ashleigh, and Allie watched, Allie's Wonder began nursing again.

AP Photo

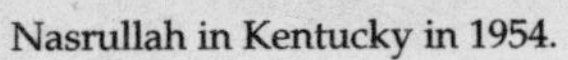

Nasrullah in Kentucky in 1954.

NASRULLAH

1940–1959

Already at the top of the sire list in England, in 1950 Nasrullah was imported from Ireland to Kentucky's prestigious Claiborne Farm. During his nine years at stud in the United States, the willful but brilliant stallion sired nine horses that were officially recognized as the champions of their divisions.

Renowned as the "sire of sires," Nasrullah, from the Darley Arabian line of Thoroughbreds, topped the North American list of sires five times. His son Bold Ruler was the top North American sire eight times. The list of the top one hundred racehorses of the twentieth century includes many of Nasrullah's descendants, including Secretariat, Seattle Slew, Alydar, Ruffian, Alysheba, Nashua, and Spectacular Bid, to name a few. In addition, his bloodlines have influenced many world-class eventing horses.

Mary Newhall spent her childhood exploring back roads and trails on horseback with her best friend. She now lives with her family and horses on Washington State's Olympic Peninsula. Mary has written novels and short stories for both adults and young adults.